Best Wishes to all my fellow BRGA residents !

Lee Taylor

THE COLLIES OF CHRISTMAS

By Ace Mask

Illustrations

by

Cindy Alvarado

https://www.facebook.com/colliesofheathercircle

Copy Editor: Rose Hutches

Cover Art: Cindy Alvarado
etsy.com/shop/pawprintsportfolio

In Memorium

KANE
(2008-2020)
The collie who changed my life.
We have loved many dogs before
and will love many more,
but there can be none to equal
our boy Kane.

CONTENTS

SEBASTIAN AND THE THREE KINGS

Slowed by age, the elderly homeless man's pace that morning was sufficient for Sebastian's short legs to keep up as he was towed along by a thin, frayed, cotton rope. The two were perfect companions, and they had become inseparable since the day the man had spotted the little shih tzu trotting along the concrete riverbed south of downtown Los Angeles, seemingly without a care in the world, confident and happy.

The old man wondered how the little guy could maintain such an upbeat attitude. The dog likely had no idea where or when he would find his next meal, he couldn't know what danger might lie around the next corner and there didn't appear to be anyone to care for him or to give him a bit of love. Those were all concerns the man had to cope with himself daily, and he asked himself if he would be doing the dog any favor by taking him on as a partner.

"Well," he thought, "maybe we could face the daily uncertainties of life together."

The only thing that would not remain uncertain, as it turned out, was love. All of the hardships they confronted grew greater each day, but his love for the small dog was far stronger than all of the physical adversity they had to endure.

He named the dog Sebastian, but he had no idea where the name came from. It simply popped into his head. It seemed a perfect big dog name for a little dog to grow into, and the dog perked up the first time the man used it. In fact, Sebastian took to the name so quickly, the man wondered if that had been his name all along.

Today, as they walked along the sidewalk that meandered through an undistinguished suburban area, the man's body bent over the handle of an overloaded shopping cart full of salvaged junk that he pushed ahead of him, his thoughts pointed toward an even darker future than he had ever contemplated before. He was not getting any younger, and he could find no one who would hire him at his age. Even the fast-food businesses were wary. A homeless man? Probably an alcoholic or a drug addict. Unreliable. A week's wages at one of those businesses wouldn't be enough to pay for more than a night's lodging at even the cheapest motel.

The charity organizations had often been there to help with the occasional meal and bed, but that had been on an extremely limited basis. Now, during the Christmas season, they had been overwhelmed with the indigent, and the number of underprivileged had grown unmanageable. Also, he hated to submit to charity. Even in his predicament he still had a sense of pride.

The lack of nourishment in recent days was now affecting his ability to think. At times his mind simply tuned out, and he would have to shake his head to clear his senses, often finding he'd been wandering aimlessly, the little dog still at his side, looking up at him with curiosity. He adjusted the old, dark, soiled, badly worn Stetson on his head as he shambled beneath a freeway overpass. He wasn't even certain where he was or where he was headed, and he hardly even noticed the intense cold that numbed his ears and nose.

His attention was abruptly aroused by the sight of two white, fast-food paper sacks blowing about on the sidewalk ahead of him. A thin, yellow sandwich wrapper poked out of the top of the larger of the two bags and waved to him like a flag, signaling to him in the breeze. He leaned down slowly, managing the sharp pain that cut through his back and gathered up the bag, rummaging through its contents.

Momentarily forgotten, Sebastian pulled at his makeshift leash and poked his head inside the smaller bag that remained. Until now, his presence had been a comfort to the old man, despite the additional responsibility a dog's companionship might have been to one in such dire straits. But Sebastian never demanded, and he seemed content to accept what meager nourishment the two comrades could scrounge with gratitude and contentment.

Inside his bag, Sebastian found only an empty paper coffee cup, and he lapped at the small stream of liquid that dribbled out.

The old man found that only paper wrappers remained in the bag he was examining, bearing traces of grease, breadcrumbs and small dabbles of cheese that had dripped from a burger that had been completely consumed.

Warily, he tossed the bag aside, then dragged himself onward, glum and directionless. Sebastian trotted alongside.

Their wandering led them off of the larger street they had been traveling onto a smaller road that wound through a sprawling suburban neighborhood, composed of one and two-story middle-class homes fronted by green, well-kept lawns.

Sebastian had never seen anything like it. Everything was clean. There was no paper or used Styrofoam scattered on the street. There were no spray-painted symbols on the walls and fences. No one was camped out between the buildings, sleeping beneath shelters made of sheets of canvas and plastic. There was no sign of life at all outside the houses.

Sure, it was still a bit early in the morning, but he thought he should have seen some sort of activity. Also, it seemed unusually quiet save for the occasional barking of a dog here and there, echoing from behind a gated back yard as they passed.

There was something else, something that seemed far more peculiar to the little dog. Many of the front yards were adorned with bright, colorful decorations and lights, many, many lights. Beautiful ornamentation was everywhere he looked. Peculiar-looking animals proudly sprouting multi-prong horns on their heads pulled elaborately designed sleds whose sole purpose, it seemed, was simply to look pretty. Here was the figure of a heavyset man with a full, white beard, dressed for winter in a suit trimmed in white fur. Over there was a small, strangely dressed character with pointed ears, who assisted the bearded man with delightfully wrapped boxes.

Sebastian had to stop to inspect a scene laid out on the lawn in front of one home because it was so different from the others. Feeling the tug at the other end of the leash, the old man allowed him. Looking down at his friend, he noticed that the dog's head was tilted to the side in an expression of great curiosity as he beheld the elaborate display spread before him.

The old man managed a meager smile.

"It's Christmas, my friend," he said. "I don't suppose you've ever experienced one of those, have you?"

Sebastian looked up at him for a moment, as if trying to understand his words, but his attention was drawn back to the tableau on the lawn.

"See," the man explained, pointing to the various figures, "those are the shepherds of the field, and surrounding them are their sheep and their cattle. And there, see those three men holding boxes? Those are the three kings. They're bringing gifts to the newborn babe in the manger."

Three kings bringing gifts. It was all too complex for Sebastian, and his head tilted further.

The old man took his time explaining the scene to the little dog, indicating the figures of Mary and Joseph, before pointing to the image of a large, exquisite star, mounted above the stable setting. The star was covered in glitter that sparkled brightly in the morning sun.

"And up there," the old man continued, "is the heavenly star that has led these people to the stable. And there, in that little manger is the baby Jesus, Sebastian. He's the reason for the season, you see."

The words themselves made no sense to Sebastian. All of the figures on the lawn, the people, the animals, none of them was real, he knew, but he sensed that all of this meant something special, the baby in the center of it all, especially.

The old man stood, lost in reverie, and his eyes clouded as he dreamed of a world in which everyone behaved a bit more like the baby in the manger.

Sebastian sniffed the air, particularly fascinated by the men with the gifts.

A sedan passed nearby, arousing the old man from his dream and reminding him that he'd better keep moving. Residents in a neighborhood like this would likely be suspicious of him if he was noticed and a call to the police would quickly follow, Christmas be damned. It would be best to find his way out of the tract to a locale where he was less likely to draw attention. He gave a slight tug to Sebastian's lead as he pushed his shopping cart forward.

The car that had just passed them pulled into the driveway and parked in front of a single-story house a block and a half ahead of the direction the two wanderers were traveling. A young man climbed from behind the steering wheel and opened the back door of the car, retrieving several large gifts as a little girl, about eight years old, hopped out of the front seat on the other side. She wore a bright, fine, holiday dress and was giggling excitedly.

The old man turned his head away from them and pulled his hat lower over his eyes as he kept moving. He tried his best to be invisible.

Sebastian was less inclined to remain unseen, wagging his tail, panting eagerly, smiling a doggy smile as they neared the strangers. Perhaps the little girl would notice him and want to play. He did so love to play with children. But alas, he and the old man hadn't been noticed.

As they passed the visitors, an aging, gray-haired lady, joyfully laughing, came out of the house to greet the man and the girl, and she wrapped her arms around them, tightly hugging each in turn. The three of them then walked arm in arm through the front door, their laughter and excited conversation soon muffled behind the door as it closed.

Sebastian had been cheered just by the sight of them. Let's have a lot more of *that*, he thought, and his trot turned into a little prance as he continued down the sidewalk next to his friend.

Heading in the direction the old man hoped would lead them out of the residential area, they passed a single-story house located behind an expansive green lawn on a corner lot. Like the other houses, this one was gaily decorated with garland and holiday lighting, but that was not what caught the old man's eye. Sitting at the curb in front was a large, black trash container. Waste pickup in this neighborhood was scheduled for the day after Christmas, and, apparently, the residents had opted to place their container out early.

After briefly surveying the area, the old man headed for the container and threw back the lid, which fell back on its hinges as he leaned inside to inventory its contents. He found it generously filled and his spirits brightened a bit at the prospect of finding something edible.

Sebastian watched him for a moment as he rummaged through the trash bin, but his attention was soon directed back to the house where they had paused. He sat on the sidewalk and cocked his head curiously, allowing the atmosphere of the moment to wash over him.

It wasn't the decorations in front that now captivated his attention. It was the activity that was going on inside. He couldn't see beyond the tall, white door in front, on which a thick pine wreath hung, profusely decorated with holiday ornaments, nor could he see clearly through the two curtained windows that faced the street. Still, he sensed there was a great deal of excitement going on in there. He could smell the faint aroma of food cooking as it wafted through the air. He could vaguely hear the delighted, high-pitched voices of young people.

Most remarkable, however, was a distinct, welcoming sense of warmth, comfort and safety that emanated from within and touched the little dog in a way he had never known before. The old man had protected and loved him in his way, but his affection was reserved. The love inside this house, Sebastian sensed, was something far different, and more than anything, if dogs can have wishes, he wished even more than he wished for food or play, that he could go inside. As he sat there, he dreamed.

Behind the door, unseen by the little dog, a lively family sat gathered around a tall, commanding fir tree, which dominated the living room and was profusely appointed with lights and dazzling ornaments. The mother and father sat on a couch smiling as they watched their two fair-haired children, a girl of eight years and a boy of six, who were eagerly and delightedly ripping brightly colored wrapping from gifts they were exchanging that morning.

Across from the children, at the base of the tree, sat three, well-behaved collie dogs, barely able to contain their excitement as they watched the activity taking place.

There was the old collie, who had recently turned twelve years old. His soft, thick, beautiful honey sable coat still shined with a luster equal to other dogs half his age, and his sweet, brown, eyes, so loving and wise, had not yet lost their sparkle, despite his age. Only his long, silver and white muzzle gave a hint to his maturity.

Next to him sat the sable-merle, six-year-old female collie, pert and bright, her dark and light brown marbling colors complemented by an elongated white star located between two spritely, attentive ears. A single, well-defined brown left eye was offset by a deep blue right eye, which, despite the contrast, conveyed an expression of unusual beauty and quiet intelligence.

The four-year-old young collie beside her sat strong and straight, his moderately wide chest thrust forward as if on purpose, projecting a sense of pride and strength. His white markings were striking against the dark mahogany coloring of his long, rich coat.

Encircling the necks and chests of all three dogs was the distinctive and luxurious downy white ruff that characterizes the breed, and each was possessed of the gentle, kind, sensitive nature for which collies are known.

It didn't take long for the children to finish opening the last of their presents, and soon they were reviewing their treasures, laughing and sharing their delight with one another. Their mother stood and started to make her way to the kitchen but was stopped by her husband, who called out to the children with a reminder. They had forgotten that there were still three more gifts to be shared.

In a flash, the children turned and rummaged through a mass of wrapping paper they had tossed behind them, and soon they located three prizes holding them high above their heads as if to tease the dogs. The three collies wagged their tails excitedly as they recognized their favorite delicacies: bone-shaped chew-treats, each tied up in a brightly colored red bow. The treats were wondrously flavored, the kind a dog could eventually devour completely after a good softening up by saliva. For the collies, there could be no tastier reward, and they eagerly but courteously accepted the goodies.

The mother smiled and resumed her walk to the kitchen and their father reclined in his chair to nurse a cup of coffee and read the morning newspaper while the children were absorbed with their gifts. The old collie and the female lowered themselves onto their stomachs and held their chewy-bones tightly between their front paws as they pulled at the bows so that they might consume their sensational snacks.

The young collie, however, moved away from the group. He was taking no chances that the other dogs might gobble up their treats and then attempt to finish off his as well. He decided to seek out a secluded spot where he could look forward to a long, leisurely morning, licking and chewing as he savored his treasure uninterrupted. He left a trail of drool on the carpet as he made his way into the father's study, where he hoped he could relax undiscovered. Once inside, he circled the middle of the carpeted floor three times before eagerly dropping to the ground.

Anxious as he was to devour his bone, he was immediately distracted by a movement, a sound, which emanated from outside the front of the house. He paused his feasting, tilted his head and stopped breathing momentarily as he attempted to determine the source of the disturbance. His hearing was sensitive enough to alert him of any front yard interlopers, whether it be the postman, the gardener, a neighbor passing by with a dog on a daily walk, or simply one of the neighborhood children seeking to retrieve a soccer ball that may have gone astray. Any of those sounds would normally jolt him into action and a bedlam of barking, but the sound outside this time was different. He rose to his feet to investigate, leaving his Christmas bone in the middle of the carpet.

Jumping onto the love seat sofa which sat in front of the lone window in the room, the young collie could easily observe the entire front yard through open shutters, and he instinctively inhaled in preparation for a flurry of barking, but the sound caught in his throat before it could escape. What he saw outside was not a threat to his territory, he sensed, and there was something mysterious in the air this morning that calmed him and assured him that the two figures out front might be friends. More than that, the young collie found himself overwhelmed with the same feeling that sometimes guided him when someone in his family needed him.

He saw the man outside in the tattered jacket leaning into the family trash container as he sorted through its contents, but his attention was captured by the little dog who sat by the curb. The two dogs simultaneously locked eyes with each other. They remained transfixed for several moments.

What was the scroungy, undersized dog doing out there in the cold when he should be indoors with his family like everyone else, the collie wondered.

How did the big, beautiful, fluffy dog get to live inside the warm, marvelous house, the other dog puzzled.

Then another thought occurred to the collie. Something was missing. He, the female, and the old collie each had a bone. The little dog should have one, too, he concluded. The scene out front wouldn't be complete without it, but where would another one come from?

In a matter of seconds, a solution presented itself as he turned his attention back to the center of the room. Of course! The bone there on the floor! If he gave that to the little dog, all would be right!

It didn't occur to him that if he gave away his bone, he would be without. He had been given a gift, and to him, that was the important thing. Now all that mattered was that his new friend should know the same joy he had experienced when he had received it. Without another thought, he leaped from the couch and scooped up the bone in his mouth, all in one smooth move as he rushed out the den door.

The collie took advantage of a little-known secret around the household. He had discovered it one day quite by accident when he had thrown himself down in front of the front door and, in so doing, his back gently pushed against it, causing it to open. The trick only worked if the door had not been locked from the inside, and fortunately for him, that was the case that morning. A gentle push with a front paw and the door opened just a crack, enough for him to pull it inward, and he dashed out, unnoticed by anyone inside.

Merrily he rushed across the lawn, the bone in his mouth, and stopped just short of Sebastian, who rose to his feet, watching in disbelief as the young collie approached.

The two dogs stood their ground a moment, each waiting for a move from the other until finally, the collie dropped the bone, and the two dogs touched noses. The big dog felt an impulse to play until he remembered his purpose in greeting the little dog, and he reached down with his nose and touched the chew-bone, nudging it toward him. Then he sat down to watch for a reaction.

Sebastian studied the object before him for a moment before sniffing it up and down. When he assured himself that this was a treat, he began licking the bone enthusiastically, as the collie watched.

Those who study such things declare that dogs don't understand the behavior of sharing. Others have cited examples that might refute that claim, but there are few to deny that dogs enjoy helping, so perhaps that was the motivation that guided the young collie that Christmas morning. Whatever the reason, Sebastian was grateful, amazed, and happy.

The old man halted his work inside the trash container and took note of the interaction between the two dogs. The collie's charity toward his little dog was something he hadn't seen performed by either animal or human for longer than he could remember. It filled his heart with happiness, and for the first time in many years, tears filled his eyes.

"Thank you, boy," he said as he lovingly patted the collie's head.

The man had little time to relish the scene, however, as he

became aware of voices close by, which indicated someone was approaching. Fearful he might be reprimanded for foraging, he closed the lid on the trash container and prepared to move on. Reaching down, he gently took the bone from Sebastian. He knew it was too large for the dog to be able to carry, and he planned to return it to him at a nearby park, where they would settle while the old man enjoyed a stale, half-eaten doughnut he had found.

"Let's go, Sebastian," he said as he laid the bone in his cart and pushed off.

Sebastian stood up on his hind feet to look after his gift and the man tugged at his makeshift leash, urging the dog to follow him.

While the two of them were walking away, the young collie was joined by the female and the old collie, who had finished devouring their chew-bones and now stood beside him. Having found the front door open, they were curious to learn what had drawn him outdoors, and they watched as the two strangers departed.

More than the separation from his bone, Sebastian regretted having to leave his new pal behind, and he walked sideways beside the old man as he looked behind him, taking in the new friend he had made.

The little dog saw them there, all three of them, as they watched him go. At that moment he made a connection. He understood everything he had seen that morning, and as he turned to travel on, he trotted along with happiness and satisfaction.

He had received a gift from The Three Kings.

Cindy Alvarado

THE SHEPHERD'S GIFT

In all of the years Andrew Duffy had been tending his flock in the Scottish Highlands, he had never lost a sheep. Not one. There was the occasional stillborn, but he had no control over that, though he cursed the fates for allowing it to occur on his watch, and he would maintain an ill-temper for days following.

There had been a time when he had been responsible for flocks many times the size of the eighty or so blackface he now drove from the hills and glens on which they had been grazing. It had been a strong blow to his pride the day Sir Charles Sinclair, the landowner by whom old Andrew was employed, sat him down and informed him he would be tending a much smaller flock than in years past. He had been a shepherd for the Sinclair family for many a year before Sir Charles had been born, and the news unsettled him, much as he was grateful that the message had been conveyed to him personally, rather than its having been relayed through the overseer. In time, however, Andrew came to realize his good fortune that he had not been replaced by a younger shepherd. It was a bitter pill to swallow nonetheless.

Though he had long acknowledged his waning strength, he was confident that his collie was more than capable of managing the sheep and getting them where they needed to be. In fact, the dog often accomplished the task with few commands from him. The "beast," as he called him, was one in a long line of dogs Andrew had mastered. With his exquisite, long, mahogany coat, he was unlike the smaller, quieter, dark dogs coming into favor with many another of his fellow shepherds trekking the Highlands at that period of the late nineteenth century. Andrew didn't care how the dog looked. He cared more about how the dog worked, and he could not have been more satisfied with his partner of choice. Man and dog were one.

The two of them had driven the sheep for some distance that day in late December before Andrew began to notice the signs of a breeding storm the like of which had not been seen in the purple moorlands of Inverness-shire since memory could serve. It was rolling in fast, and the danger it posed for the shepherd and his flock was not to be winked at. Rising to his feet, he uttered a quiet command under his breath.

"Away to me," he said, and Robbie, who lay nearby, watching over the sheep grazing before him, responded instantaneously, flanking to the back of the flock to gather them.

The collie had been conscious of the impending blizzard long before his superintendent and had only been waiting for a command in the form of a whistle or a word to drive the flock from the heights to the hollows, back to the shepherd's cottage and shelter in the valley, where they could wait out the freezing hell that was surely on its way.

The moment the dog stood, his thick, marvelous coat bristling in the wind, the sheep began moving as one. They had been under Robbie's charge all of their lives, and more often than not, they would respond to his authority with little resistance. That day, however, a ewe was proving to be consistently contrary, stubbornly moving away from the rest of the flock toward a rocky area amid the hills where she had tried to settle by herself. Andrew and his collie both recognized the signs. She had set her eyes on a lonely spot to give birth.

The shepherd cursed himself as the ewe contentiously turned to face his dog. Lambing season was normally expected in January or February, but he recalled discovering a cursed ram had managed to jump his pen in July, and as chance would have it, he found the one ewe that happened to be cycling and ready to accept a ram. Andrew should have noticed the signs of the impending birth before he had left his cottage the day before.

If the ewe gave birth soon, she could potentially be a problem if assistance were needed. He knew he could rely on Robbie to corner her, and the collie would likely even be capable of tipping her to the ground and holding her there, but Andrew's declining strength might not be sufficient to pull a twisted or oversized lamb from the birth canal by its front ankles if needed.

A man of his experience should have noticed that her bag had looked a little heavy, he now considered. Being in a meditative mood, however, he had unintentionally wandered into the upper pasturelands the day before, higher and farther than normal for this time of year. When belated by nightfall, he had decided it was too late to start back home, so he shared what remained in his water-butt with Robbie before curling up in the moss-flow of a rocky hillside. With only his plaid for a coverlet, he read a few verses from the well-worn Bible he kept with him at all times and then allowed himself to drift off to sleep, leaving Robbie to tend the flock. Andrew had spent many a night in that manner, but never without planning. That night he had allowed his thoughts and his reason to be clouded by a troublesome conclusion he had come to accept: His life would soon be over.

On that day, as the storm approached, there could be no sleep outdoors. He and his dog had eaten the last bit of food he had brought along, and now they were hungry, cold and exhausted, though Robbie showed little sign of wear as he faced off the obstinate ewe that finally, yet reluctantly, joined the rest of the flock. As the sheep moved, however, and as Robbie rushed from flank to flank, keeping them in close array, the ewe required constant correction as she continually attempted to break ranks.

Andrew followed not far behind, only peripherally aware of his flock, his eyes cast downward, his uneven stride assisted by his shepherd's crook. The ache in his chest that had grown increasingly painful in recent months had become unbearable, and all of the effort he had made to disregard its presence was now impossible. This would be his final trek to the fields he loved so dearly, he knew, but he felt no remorse. Death is but a part of life, and he was ready to accept his fate without regret and without fear.

It was Robbie he worried about. Robbie would understand his passing, as all of God's creatures seem to understand, but Robbie would mourn. Andrew was sure of that. He remembered the story of Greyfriar's Bobby, the beloved little terrier of an Edinburgh policeman, who remained at the graveside of his beloved master for fourteen loyal years. That would be Robbie, he knew. Of all the dogs Andrew had known in his long life, Robbie was the best and the dearest.

For many weeks, the collie had been aware of his master's condition. Robbie didn't know exactly what it was, but he knew there existed an Unknown Thing somewhere deep within the one he loved as his god, and he sensed that it would soon take him away. It was a distraction for him, but he never let it hinder his responsibilities. Not a single sheep was allowed to stray (though the tiresome ewe tested his tolerance), and those old enemies, the fox and the eagle, were always kept at a distance. Now the Unknown Thing was a new enemy against which he must remain vigilant, though he was uncertain how.

Dusk was settling in, and the first few flakes were floating from the sky, whipped about by a biting, bitterly cold wind as the shepherd and his collie approached their small cottage. All indications were that within hours the land would be smothered with snowdrifts, deep and impenetrable.

Along the way, Andrew began to question if he had the strength to make it home. An idea had occurred to him, and the more he contemplated the notion, the more he was energized. By the time he opened the gate to the sheep pen and Robbie made sure they were all gathered inside beneath the thatch-covered cote, Andrew had made a decision that brightened his soul against the darkness in which it had been engulfed.

Before he could close the gate, the damnable ewe made one last leap for independence, pushing through the small opening left to her, catching him off guard and off balance and knocking him to the ground as she muscled her way through.

Robbie was ready for her and stopped her in her tracks as he backed her up, barking fiercely in her face. The ewe was not to be denied, however, and stiffly stopped in place, angrily stomping a front hoof at the dog. With much effort, Andrew picked himself up and held the gate closed to prevent any other sheep from escaping and then watched as the ewe made two quick passes at the collie, her head lowered to butt him aside. But Robbie was too quick and too experienced for her, and in a swift move, he flew in low toward her and nipped an ankle before making a roundabout move to stand before her again, his bark becoming more threatening. For a moment the two stood in a face-off as the ewe considered her options.

Making sure the flock was gathered together at the back of the pen, Andrew flung wide the gate and in the same move, struck the ground in front of the ewe fiercely with his crook, as Robbie leaped toward her and gave her a quick hit on the nose with his mouth, not a bite, really, but more of a bump. The combined sudden moves from the team startled the ewe enough to turn her around and send her swiftly scurrying into the midst of the huddled flock. Andrew promptly slammed the gate behind her and lowered the latch to secure it.

Such an adventure might have laid Andrew low had his heart not been beating strongly at the idea he had been formulating as they had approached the cottage. He felt better than he had felt for many weeks, and he nodded for Robbie to follow him inside.

" 'Tis Christmas Eve, Robbie!" Andrew announced inside as he closed the door behind him, tossed his tam aside and leaned his crook against the wall.

The single-room cottage was completely bereft of ornamentation and consisted only of a table and two chairs, a well-worn armchair pulled up before the fireplace and a cupboard stocked with scant provisions and cooking utensils. A well-worn, straw-filled mattress atop a wooden bedstead positioned against a wall provided minimal comfort.

Scrounging through his provisions, Andrew found a small pot containing the remains of a vegetable stew he had prepared two days previously, and he set it on the floor, where Robbie consumed its contents within moments.

"They'll be a meal like no' ya ever had 'afore, in a wee bit," Andrew said to the dog, who looked up at him quizzically from the pot he had been licking. He often carried on long conversations with the dog, and he was near certain every word was understood.

"Aye," he said in response to the dog's look. " 'Tis Christmas Eve, ye sh'd know. Might well hae meself a ni' Ay'll remember fer wot time is to come."

Robbie cocked his head, and the old man gave him a wink as he threw his tam back on his head and grabbed his crook before reaching for the door.

" 'Mon," he commanded, and the dog followed him out.

A small village was but an hour distant, past the manor house of Sir Charles, and even in his disabled condition and though the snowfall was gaining density, Andrew was determined to make his way in less time than that. As he set his path in that direction, Robbie hesitated when he realized they were not going to check on the sheep. Stopping midway between the cabin and the sheep's pen, he called after his master with a bark.

"She'll not lamb fr a few hours yet, so you needn't be feart," Andrew called back to him over his shoulder. "But bide here if ye must, dug. As fr me, Ay'm away fr dauner."

Robbie watched him continue his way, torn between his duty to the sheep and his obedience to the shepherd. The bothersome ewe was pacing the fence of the enclosure, looking for an escape. It wasn't until Andrew yelled a last, " 'Mon, dug!" that the collie followed after, slowly at first, then at a trot to catch up with him.

The Crook and Boot Tavern was located amid several small shops in the simple little village. Bright, welcoming light radiated through the large window and the lively voices that merrily emanated from within warmed the heart of the old shepherd, who had been made quite weary from the strain of his walk. Making his way inside, Robbie following, he returned the greeting extended by the few acquaintances he recognized amid the two dozen or so regulars who were gathered about the room. He found himself a table near the wall, and feeling the pain in his chest returning with a vengeance, he carefully seated himself and removed his tam as Robbie, still fretting about the belligerent ewe, lay himself down at his foot.

"Andrew Duffy!" exclaimed the proprietor with a hearty greeting. "We've na seen yer bahooky in here since I cannot remember when. What now brings ya down from the hillside?"

Andrew slapped a coin down on the table.

"A bottle, if ye please, Brody Mackenzie," he said. "Y'r very best'll be fine enough."

Brody stood back for a moment, studying the shepherd's face. He had known Andrew longer than he could remember, and though the old man's appearance at the tavern had become less frequent in recent years, he could still claim a lasting companionship that the infrequency of those visits could not erode. He knew his friend well enough by simply looking into his face that he was not at all well.

Nevertheless, Brody knew better than to launch immediately into intimate questions about health and fate.

"The best and no less!" he exclaimed and headed to the counter, where he grabbed a bottle of whiskey from the shelf. Sweeping up a glass with his free hand, he caught the eye of his wife, Maggie, who was merrily pouring a glass nearby, and he nodded toward his friend. She followed his gesture, and, seeing Andrew's face, her expression turned to a frown of concern as she acknowledged his condition.

Grabbing the bottle and glass from her husband, she picked up an additional glass from the counter and approached Andrew, who was staring with a distant look at the dog lying at his feet. Robbie was resting his head on his master's boot, a forlorn look on his face. She set down the bottle and glasses between them and reached for a half-eaten plate of roast beef from a table nearby, which she tossed in front of the dog. He attacked the dish ravenously.

"Merry Christmas, Andrew Duffy," Maggie said with a comforting voice as she poured two drinks and shoved one of them toward him.

"Aye. Same to you," he replied before downing his drink.

"Is this how ye'll be passin' the time this Yuletide, then?" she asked.

"Aye," he nodded, pouring himself another glass. "Jest me an' the beast there at mah foot. Same's I been passin' the Yuletide these many years now since m'dear Mary's passin' so long ago."

"No relations? No friends?"

"No relatives t' speak of. Mah friends are all here tonight," he nodded toward the center of the tavern. "Sheep are in the pen, and yer sittin' 'cross from me. Nobody else. Robbie's as good a friend as a soul could hope for anyway. That'll dae."

Robbie, licking the last morsel from the plate before him, raised his head at the sound of his name.

"Blessin's of the Season to ye then," Maggie said, raising her glass in a toast.

Wincing with pain, Andrew returned the salute and filled

his glass again.

"Noo, jist haud on!" she cautioned him, raising her hand. "Ye'll soon be hammered, and the night still young."

"Aye, and Ay'll be mad wi' it soon enough. I'm fair puckled, Maggie. I don't mind tellin' ye."

Maggie was about to question him when they were joined by a tall man with a neatly trimmed brown beard. He held a glass of whiskey in one hand, a walking stick in the other. He was immaculately dressed, and the cut of his expensive suit immediately informed the locals he was a wealthy gentleman and not from these parts. Robbie, always quick to judge character and never wrong in his assessments, was annoyed straight off and wished he would go away.

"Excuse me, sir. Ma'am," the man interrupted with a slight bow to Andrew and a nod to Maggie. The enunciation of each spoken word identified him as a Londoner and quite possibly a peer of the realm.

"I do hope you'll forgive my intrusion," he said with a slight smile. "I couldn't help but overhear. Am I correct in assuming I am addressing Andrew Duffy, drover and employee of Sir Charles Sinclair?"

"Aye, that wu'd be me," Andrew replied, downing another whiskey.

"I wonder, ..." he began as he grabbed a chair from a nearby table and gestured to the empty spot across from Andrew. "May I?"

"How no. 'Tis Christmas Eve. Why not?"

"I'd best be helpin' me Brody with the pourin' o' the drinks," Maggie said, as she stood and headed for the bar. "We'll pick up where we left off in a wee bit, Andrew."

Before he sat, the Englishman offered his hand to the

shepherd.

"Merry Christmas to you, sir. I am Lord Agnew," he announced.

Grimacing with pain, Andrew weakly shook his hand, and the man sat.

"I'm a guest of Sir Charles, Mister Duffy, and I must tell you he speaks very highly of you," the visitor claimed as he carefully placed his glass on the table.

" 'Deed," Andrew acknowledged.

"Indeed," Lord Agnew confirmed with a simulated smile. "More particularly, he speaks very highly of your collie dog, this beauty right here, in fact."

He glanced under the table at Robbie. The dog knew he was part of the dialogue between the two men, though he couldn't understand the words. Andrew made no response as he continued to drink.

"You see, sir, I own a kennel at my estate near Birmingham, which specializes in the exhibition, field competition and breeding of the finest champion dogs in all of Britain. Forgive me for being immodest, but the quality of my dogs is quite beyond compare."

"Mae hat's off t'ye," Andrew replied.

"Yes. I am presently endeavoring to enrich my kennel with the rough collie breed, and in that effort, I am seeking the very finest in intelligence, temperament and conformation."

The Englishman realized he was having little luck in acquiring the shepherd's interest.

"And in that perspective," he continued, "I have a business proposition for you."

"Business!" Andrew snorted.

"Your collie, here. He has quite a reputation in this region.

Sir Charles himself has told me that he holds him in very high regard."

"Ye speakin' o' Robbie here, are ya?"

"Robbie. Indeed, yes."

"Well, he's the best Ay've ever shared a plaid with of a night, that's fer shore."

"May I?" Lord Agnew began, pointing the tip of his walking stick at Robbie. "Would you be good enough to command your dog to stand? I should very much like to observe his structure, if I may."

Robbie knew he was being commanded to rise, but there was only one individual to whom he would respond, and he looked to that individual for confirmation.

Andrew observed the Englishman through a squinted eye but did not acknowledge the request.

"You see, sir," Lord Agnew explained, "I am prepared to make you a very generous offer for your dog here if I like what I see. A *very* generous offer."

The conversation at Andrew's table had been overheard by several of the patrons in the tavern, and they began to gather around the two men and the dog. They had no doubt Andrew would never entertain any impulse to sell his collie, but they were curious as to just how this meeting would play out. Lord Agnew looked nervously around at the gathering.

"Mister Duffy," he said, clearing his throat and lowering his voice to a near whisper, "I am prepared to offer you a very sizeable sum of money for your animal. Forgive me for pointing this out, but Sir Charles has informed me you are not in the very best of health. Given your age, there is a strong likelihood that your days as a shepherd will soon be nearing an end if they haven't already. The offer I am prepared to make for your dog will be more than sufficient to allow you to live your final days in comfort and pleasure."

Bill Ferguson, a tall, thin, aging, fellow shepherd and longtime friend of Andrew's, started to speak.

"Sir," he began, "Ye got ta be an eejit fer shore if ye think a shepherd wud ... "

Andrew held up his hand to silence him.

"Comfort, ye say?" Andrew said, addressing the Englishman. "Pleasure, ye say? Tell me, sar, wud ye put a price on yer own brother fer comfort? Fer pleasure?"

"Well," replied Lord Agnew, sweat forming on his brow, "of course I wouldn't. But Mister Duffy, we're only talking about a *dog* here."

Andrew, having been sitting slumped in his chair, now painfully sat up straight, and his face, which had been drained of color, now turned a vivid shade of red. Simultaneously, the group around the table closed in menacingly.

"*Only a dug?*" hissed Andrew.

Lord Agnew recognized how badly he had handled what he thought was going to be a very simple business transaction: quick in, quick out. He hastened to make one final attempt.

"Wait, sir," he said in a tremulous voice. "I apologize to you. I profusely apologize for failing to acknowledge the bond between you and this creature, which you very obviously hold sacred. But, please, consider this: When that day finally arrives when you have, shall we say, 'shuffled off this mortal coil,' what is to become of your dog? Don't you see? In my kennel he will receive, for the remainder of his life, care worthy of a king. My kennel staff will see to his every need. Medical, food, grooming. Who could give your dog more? Who will look after your dog when you are gone?"

"Oh, there's no worry on that count, yer lordship, sir," Maggie's voice was heard loudly from behind. The group moved back to allow her to approach more closely.

"There'll be no shortage o' friends o' Andrew Duffy t' see after his dug when that necessity shud arrive, ye can be shore o' that. No shortage o' shepherds thet wud give Robbie the life he lives for, carin' f'r the blackface sheep in the Highlands, 'stead o' spendin' the rest of his life wastin' away in some kennel up north, pampered an' primped and mis'rable."

"Aye," the assembled group agreed vocally.

The visitor's standing with Andrew and his friends was now readily apparent to Robbie, who stood and faced the bearded man. Though menace was rarely a trait the dog was called upon to display, intimidation was now his demeanor.

"Look at that form!" Lord Agnew could not resist remarking. Then with a shrug, he bid the assemblage a reluctant good day, tossed a coin on the table, gathered his hat and coat, and after one last look of regret at Robbie, he made his exit.

"That'll dae, Robbie," Andrew said to his dog, who returned to his place of comfort at his feet.

The group surrounding the table disbursed, and Maggie again seated herself by Andrew. She laid her hand across his and drew near.

"Now," Maggie asked softly, "tell me wut's ailin' ye, 'cause 'tis plain t' ever'one, 'cludin' Robbie there, that ye belong home in yer bed."

Andrew's breathing was labored, and his eyes grew heavy. He attempted to wave her away. He barely managed a reply.

" 'Tis over, Maggie. 'Tis over."

Robbie jumped to his feet as his master slumped forward.

Andrew's head fell to the table with its full weight, tipping the whiskey bottle on the way. Maggie grabbed the bottle in mid-spill.

Several in the room rushed over to their friend.

"Doctor McClure!" Maggie called out to a short, pudgy gent seated in a corner nearby. Quickly sizing up the situation, the man seized his medical satchel and rushed to the side of the stricken shepherd as the others made room for him to pass. No one was certain how he had qualified to become a doctor, but he was the only practicing medical professional in the area, certified or otherwise, and everyone trusted him.

Two men lifted Andrew into a sitting position as the doctor quickly retrieved a stethoscope from his bag and pulled back the clothing from around Andrew's neck and sought to analyze his heartbeat.

All was silent except for the painfully raspy sound of Andrew's breathing as Doctor McClure moved the bell of his stethoscope about his chest. At length, he redirected his attention to Andrew's eyes as he pulled back his eyelids to determine consciousness. Then, with a long exhale of breath, the doctor stood and removed his stethoscope, slowly shaking his head.

The tension drained from everyone in the room and was replaced by an invisible cloud of gloom. The only sound to be heard, save for Andrew's agonized breathing, was a soft whine coming from Robbie, who was nudging his muzzle beneath his master's unresponsive arm.

Holding back tears, Maggie signaled to Bill Ferguson and a couple of men standing at his side.

"Geeza haun, Bill," she ordered as she moved to lift Andrew from the table. "We'll get him t' the bed in the back."

Suddenly, Andrew stirred.

"No! No!" he pleaded as he struggled for breath. "Hame. Get me hame. I got a ewe. She's aboot to lamb. Aside, I want t' die in mae own bed."

As quickly as he had come to, he lost consciousness once more, and as Maggie released her hold on his shoulders, he again collapsed forward. Robbie managed to lay his head in Andrew's lap under the table.

The gathering looked to Maggie for further instruction as she stood, considering her options. Finally, she nodded.

"Right then," she said with a sigh. " 'Tis only proper he shu'd be wantin' to die in his own bed."

"Mah wagon is out front," Ferguson volunteered as he headed to the door. "Ye lads give me a hand an' we'll git him to his cottage."

"Ayle be goin' wi' ye," Maggie said.

"Now hold there," Brody interrupted, making his way from behind the counter. "There'll not be a one o' ye goin' out on a night like this. An' Christmas Eve t' boot! Jist get him to the bed in back and ... "

"Haud yer wheesht, Brody," Maggie countered, "and git yer bahooky back b'hind th' counter! We'll be takin' Andrew Duffy hame now, and there's an end to 't!"

Brody shook his head as he threw his hands up in the air. He knew that an argument with his wife was not a winning proposition.

"One o' ye fetch Father McClannon," he said to a man nearby. "See if he'll meet ye at Andrew's cottage. This weather, I wud by doubtin' it, tho."

One of the men obliged, grabbing his hat and coat on the way out.

Robbie raced in circles around Andrew's limp form as two other men lifted his arms over their shoulders and attempted to walk him toward the door. Another individual held his legs when it was determined that his dragging feet made transport difficult.

"Step aside, Robbie m'boy!" Maggie said, waving him away. "We'll be takin' 'm hame noo."

The tone of her voice appeased the dog, and he circled and trailed behind.

The crew was soon outside, and Maggie smoothed out an old blanket in the back of Ferguson's wagon before the men lay Andrew down. Brody soon joined them and spread two blankets he had gotten from the back room over him, then turned and assisted Maggie as she slipped into her coat.

"Haste ye back," he said, as he hugged his wife. "I still say yer daft t' be out on a night like this. An' Christmas Eve t' boot!"

"Yer repeatin' yerself," Maggie replied. "Now get back to mindin' th' tavern. Ay'll be back soon enuf."

Brody reluctantly assisted her onto the bench next to Ferguson, who handed her a blanket to toss over her lap. Glancing over her shoulder to ensure that Andrew was comfortable and secure, it did not surprise her to see that Robbie was snuggled close beside him, his cheek nuzzled next to his master's.

A brisk snap of the reins and Ferguson's horse and wagon and its passengers quickly disappeared into the darkness and the cold, thick, flurry of sleet and snow.

The road traveled lay unseen beneath a bewildering, ever-thickening white blanket. Ferguson managed his best to navigate by the few bits of landscape he could discern, but the elements concealed most, and even with Maggie's coaching, several wrong turns required back-tracking to correct course. Twice the wheels of the wagon veered into a ditch, requiring the two of them to disembark and painfully lift the cart onto flat ground.

After nearly forty-five minutes of hit-and-miss, trial-and-error and misadventure, when they should have nearly reached their destination, Ferguson pulled his horse to a halt and stepped to the ground. Nervously glancing at Maggie, he attempted to lead the animal afoot, but it was to no avail. Eventually, he came to a stop.

" 'Tis no use, Bill!" Maggie called down to him. "We'll never make it, and at this rate, we're sure t' freeze t' death long 'afore!"

"Aye," he agreed. "Problem is, I got no idea which way t' go t' get us back whar we come from."

For the moment, the two of them remained still, minds and bodies becoming increasingly numb in the unrelenting cold. A decision had to be made soon.

Robbie's head popped up from his reclining position next to his master. He knew where they were headed, and he knew that the reason had to do with Andrew's weakened condition, but he couldn't understand why they had stopped. After a quick read of Maggie and Ferguson's body language, he understood. It was a problem the shepherd and his flock had faced a couple of times in their work together, and in those instances, the collie, with his cunning and experience, had managed to guide them safely home. He comprehended that his skill was needed again, and he leaped from the wagon and trotted to a position in front of Ferguson and his horse, where he stood and peered into the silent darkness that lay before them.

There was little for the dog to ascertain by scent and even less to be determined visually, but even with both of those senses camouflaged by the snow, Robbie could still make better use of them than any human. He was also possessed of an uncanny sense of direction, and it was this ability that prompted him forward, veering slightly to the right.

Ferguson nodded as he vaulted back into his wagon and gave a wink to Maggie.

"He'll get us there. No time!"

The route Robbie followed was quick and direct, and even with his pace hindered by the sluggishness of the horse and wagon that followed him, the gray outline of Andrew's small cottage was soon in sight.

As Ferguson pulled his horse to a stop, Maggie rushed to the cabin door and held it wide to permit them to lug Andrew inside. Robbie paused long enough to ensure that his master was in caring hands before he turned his attention to the pen.

The sheep stood huddled close together, shielded from the storm beneath the shelter, but the collie knew immediately that all was not well. He rushed to the gate.

The wooden latch on the gate was in place, as Andrew had left it when they had departed for the tavern but the bottom corner of the gate was bent slightly outward as if forced by something within. The hard-headed ewe, as Robbie feared, had managed an escape and was now undoubtedly making her way back to the spot in the Highlands where she was determined to give birth.

Robbie could still faintly make out the ewe's odor, but what remained would soon disappear beneath the steadily falling snow. At first, he started to follow the trail but suddenly stopped. He had to somehow convey to his master that he was leaving but that Andrew must wait for his return, for all would be made well again when every member of the flock was safely gathered.

Rushing back to the cottage, he nudged open the door that was never locked. Andrew, still unconscious, was on his bed, attended by Ferguson and Maggie. Robbie's heart sank at the sight of his god, helpless and barely alive.

The dog approached the side of the bed, laying his head on the old, worn pillow that supported the dying man's head. Robbie wished he would open his eyes, if even for one last time. If his master could see him, if he looked into his face, he was sure he would understand why he had to leave him for a while. The two of them had always comprehended what the other was thinking, without having to utter a sound, so intertwined had their understanding of one another merged through the years.

Robbie recognized that Andrew would be leaving him soon, and that knowledge moved him to action. Lifting his head, he licked his master on the cheek, then turned and pushed against the door, which opened wide enough for him to nudge it open, and he was gone. The collie was not in the habit of licking, but Andrew would sometimes playfully encourage him to "give a kiss," and the dog would reluctantly oblige. This time he had needed no prompting. This time it was shared from the heart.

"Where wud he be goin' at a time like this?" Maggie wondered aloud.

"Ah dinnae ken," Ferguson answered, "but 'aye feart we willnae be seein' him again." Then, shaking his head, he headed for the door.

"Aye best be gettin' th' horse t' the shelter," he said on his way out.

Outside the door, Ferguson could make out the dog's paw prints in the snow as they headed away from the cottage. As he removed his horse's harness and led him to the shelter, he noticed the gap at the bottom of the gate and he immediately understood.

Robbie did not return that night, nor did he return the next day. It had been his life's work to serve the one person he loved more than anything on earth, and Maggie was certain he had perished in pursuit of his duty. She knew that he would have given no thought to the danger that presented.

Andrew did not survive the night. Shortly before midnight that Christmas Eve, his hand moved down to the side of his bed, as if reaching out to touch his devoted dog one last time and, failing to find him there, his hand dropped and he breathed his last.

Christmas Day was still and quiet, and the winter sun shone brightly as Maggie and Ferguson silently set out for the village. Before leaving the cottage, they had gently placed Andrew's body in the back of the wagon, and as they covered him with blankets, Maggie noticed the edge of his worn Bible, sticking out of his pocket. Removing it, she thumbed through the pages and then carried it with her as she mounted the bench next to Ferguson. She read many verses aloud as they traveled. She knew Andrew would have wished it.

They made good time, stopping only at the manor house briefly to inform Sir Charles of Andrew's passing and to enable him to dispatch a man from his stable to tend to the sheep.

"He was a man of noble character," Sir Charles said with bowed head. "And I know of no other shepherd who could match his claim for never having lost a single sheep from his flock."

"Aye," Maggie said. "But I regret t' inform ye that today one may be missin'. His collie left in the blizzard last night t' fetch it, but I'm afraid th' poor creature perished in the effort."

"Robbie?" Sir Charles reacted with surprise. "Then your news is doubly grievous. I doubt the poor dog could have survived for long without the man he loved so dearly."

Two days later Sir Charles and his wife as well as their guest, Lord Agnew, joined the entire village as they gathered in the small church in the village to say goodbye to Andrew in a service presided over by Father McClannon. The priest made up for his inability to be present at the shepherd's deathbed by delivering a eulogy that was genuine and heartfelt.

" 'Tis hard to picture our dear friend alone, without his dog," he said at one point, veering from his prepared words. Those gathered muttered in agreement.

"Oh," he hastily added, "he's with our Lord and Savior now, of course, but I can't help thinking that maybe Robbie is also there, at his side. If that's so, then maybe, just maybe, heaven is made just a wee bit happier for Andrew Duffy."

Father McClannon cast a quick, humble, apologetic glance upward and concluded with, "Forgive me, Lord."

Sir Charles had covered all expenses for Andrew's service as well as the cost of burial. He also intended to pay for a sizeable headstone to be placed at the gravesite where the congregation gathered to say goodbye.

It was there, as a lone piper piped farewell and the priest was delivering a final prayer, that a sound was heard at the cemetery gate, silencing them both, and those standing at the back of the assemblage turned to discern the source of the distraction.

It was the unmistakable sound of a lamb, not three days old, scrambling to catch up to its mother as she was herded from behind toward the gravesite. Those in the front of the group also turned and, upon doing so, they beheld the ewe and her lamb. They widened a path to make way for them and for the collie who followed a short distance behind.

Robbie was worn and ragged, and he traveled slowly, with his head hung low, but he was determined to deliver the last of the flock to the man he loved. As the lamb suckled her, the ewe nibbled a patch of grass sticking up through the snow nearby. The collie collapsed before the coffin of his master.

In all of the years Andrew Duffy had been tending his flock in the Scottish Highlands, he had never lost a sheep. Not one.

THE CHRISTMAS DRESS

Micah Hanes was mentally adding the money he'd been saving since he started working at the train depot in the small Mississippi town in which he lived. It wasn't very much money, especially considering the back-breaking work he had done to earn it, but for a twelve-year-old African American boy living in the deep South in the year 1909, $3.5O seemed a fortune.

Several months earlier, his mother had paused to admire a dress that was displayed in the front window of the dry goods store where she shopped in the black-owned-businesses area of town. Micah had rarely seen her pay any attention to anything for herself, but somehow the simple garment had caught her off guard, and for a brief moment she allowed herself to fantasize. Just as quickly, she tossed aside her foolish daydream and hastened into the establishment, where she intended to buy a few yards of inexpensive fabric with which to make Micah's younger sister a new shirt. She needed to replace the tattered one she had been wearing to school for far too long.

Micah lingered behind to try to understand what it was about the dress in the window that had captured his mother's attention. Even at his young age, he could see there was nothing at all fancy about it. He judged it to be pretty simple in all aspects. Of course, if it had been anything fancy, she would never have given it a second look. Ostentation was not in her character. But she needed a new dress, and at that moment he was determined to get it for her. Besides, he concluded, that dress would look a sight better on his mother than it did on the dummy in the window. Christmas would be coming along in a few months, he reasoned, and if he could land a small paying job, any job at all would do, he estimated he just might be able to afford to buy it. Wouldn't she be surprised? And so proud!

He had hoped to find a better paying job than the one he finally landed at the train depot, but it was the best someone of his age and race could hope for, and as Christmas approached, he resigned himself to the hard, thankless work he was assigned.

Then, on one ordinary day during school winter break, as Micah performed his tasks on the dock of the depot, an extraordinary thing occurred that would unexpectedly change his life.

"What y'all been doin' with all that money they been givin' you, boy?" asked Roy Noerdlinger with a disdainful grin as he munched on an apple. "Been investin' it in Hershey bars or givin' it to Parthy to let ya kiss her on the lips?"

Roy, four years Micah's senior, never spoke to him unless it was to put him down, and he never passed up that opportunity when the lad was compensated or on that rare occasion when he was commended for his work. Lounging on a large wooden crate that sat shoved against a wall facing the railroad receiving dock, the bully was more inclined to slap Micah on the back of the head than offer any words of praise.

Micah had been transporting a suitcase twice his size to a wagon on the dock and paused as the stationmaster handed him a few coins in passing. He deposited his week's wages into his pocket.

"Y'all'd be worth a lot more if you spent as much time working as you do bullying that boy," the stationmaster said as he tossed Roy a coin.

"You sayin' I ain't worth as much as a colored boy, Mister Shanley?" Roy responded, his voice cracking in disbelief.

"The eleven fifteen will be here any minute," the stationmaster said as he continued down the landing. "Better get off that lazy butt o' yours and get ready to do some work around here for a change."

Roy frowned as he watched him go and angrily tossed his apple core onto the railroad track. He spit on the ground beside him and directed his attention back to Micah.

"Y'all ain't answered mah question, boy," he reminded him.

"Been savin' my money to buy my momma a dress for Christmas," Micah replied as he resumed lugging the suitcase.

"What you mammy be needin' a new dress for?" Roy asked. "She's a school teacher, ain't she? Don't she waste her time teaching all them little colored kids at that schoolhouse?"

"She's not wastin' her time," Micah responded angrily as he struggled to lift the suitcase onto the wagon.

"Yeah, well, them little fuzzy-heads ain't got no brains. Ever'body knows that. Wastin' her time."

Micah clenched his teeth and reached for the push-broom leaning against the wall next to Roy. He knew there was no point in trying to defend himself against slurs from a white boy like him. It would only end in more slurs and the all-too-common slap to his head or perhaps something even worse. Roy was just jealous because Micah, without even trying, often made him look bad, and because, despite his younger age, he tended to stick to business. Roy's lack of motivation was a constant source of irritation among the other train station staff.

"Look lively, now, boy," Roy said, looking down the tracks as a train whistle blew in the distance. "Here comes the 'leven fifteen."

Micah put away his broom and prepared to assist with the unloading of the bags and freight that could be expected to arrive.

The ground trembled as the huge steam engine pulled to a stop beneath the shelter of the depot, and for a moment its massive vapor enveloped the station in smoke and heat. Porters hastened to open doors and place portable steps before each doorway while people on the platform awaiting the train rose from their benches. Micah hastened to the baggage car, tugging a sluggish luggage wagon behind him.

A large, heavyset, distinguished-looking man stepped from the doorway of one of the coaches and started to address a conductor who failed to notice and scurried down the line to tend to other passengers. The man, in his mid-fifties, elegantly dressed and clean-shaven, began looking about for assistance and tried to capture the eye of Roy, who was lighting a cigarette as he leaned against a doorway several feet away.

"You! Boy!" the man called out, waving a fedora, but Roy failed to notice.

Micah happened to be passing at the moment the man's patience reached its breaking point.

"Here! You!" the man said in a thick Southern accent, holding his hand out to stop him. "I need your assistance with an important piece of freight. Come with me, boy."

Without waiting for an acknowledgment, the man stepped from the coach door and walked swiftly toward the baggage car near the rear of the train as Micah did his best to keep up.

Reaching his destination, the man pounded on the side of the car.

"Hello in there!" he called out.

Momentarily, the coach door was slid aside from within, and a meek-looking freight clerk leaned out.

"Oh, you!" he said before retreating to more respectful comportment. "One moment, sir. I'll have him out here in a jiffy."

"Did he travel well?" the man asked. "Did you make sure he had plenty of clean, fresh water?"

Before the clerk could reply, a short, simply dressed man rushed forward.

"You're late. What kept you?" the man on the dock demanded.

"I'm so sorry, Colonel Burke," the plain dressed man apologized. "I had several things to finish up at the kennel. I know you want ever'thing clean and ready for … "

"Never mind," the Colonel interrupted brusquely. "Get up there and give that man a hand."

A ramp was lowered to the dock from the freight car, and the kennel assistant scurried aboard as his employer yelled after him.

"Get that animal out of the crate. Set him free. He must be suffocating. Hurry along, there!"

Micah moved his wagon near the base of the ramp in anticipation of the delivery and stood, waiting, next to Colonel Burke, who noticed him and smiled very slightly.

"You're going to be seeing something the like of which you've never seen before, boy," the man said with an air of condescension, "and likely never will again. Not in these parts, anyway."

The youngster's mind was crowded with fantastic images as he tried to imagine what sort of creature this dignified man had brought with him. A horse? Maybe a racehorse? A wild animal? A tiger, perhaps? He knew it was not his place to ask the big man who stood above him, almost chuckling as he watched for his reaction.

There was a long wait as the two men in the coach struggled to open a piece of freight. The muffled sound of the kennel assistant's voice could be heard as he ordered the freight clerk to assist him.

"The gate's been nailed shut!" the assistant could be heard to exclaim. "Get me a crowbar!"

The smile on the Colonel's face promptly gave way to a frown.

"What in God's name?"

The crack and creak of splintered wood generated from within as the two men loosened the nails on the crate until finally one of them could be heard breathing a heavy sigh of relief as the gate was opened, its hinges squeaking noisily.

"There we go," the clerk said.

An instant later, as if someone had turned on a brilliant ray of bright light, there stood at the top of the ramp, framed by the doorway, an animal who was, indeed, "the like of which" Micah had never seen before. His jaw went slack as he gazed upon the most beautiful image he had ever beheld.

The Colonel smiled again, and his face beamed.

"Yes!" he said under his breath.

It was a dog, of that much Micah felt fairly certain, but it was nothing at all like the hounds, the coon dogs or the mixed-breed curs that milled about town or even like the pampered, perfumed, little white dandy lap-dog Missus Hodgkins carried with her everywhere she went.

The dog (he wondered if it could even be classified as such) stood straight and grand above all, like royalty surveying his domain, and the Colonel's chest puffed out proudly as he evaluated his prize. Dominating and proud, the collie wore an expression of great dignity emphasized by a long prominent muzzle, and his brown, almond-shaped eyes conveyed superior intelligence. His ears stood tall and attentive, while the points atop each tipped forward. His long, sable coat reflected the light like brilliant gold and was offset with a breathtakingly luminescent, white ruff, which surrounded his neck like that of an imperial lion, accentuating a deep, strong chest that was held with majestic pride and strength. While he stood about 26 inches tall at his shoulder, his bearing gave the impression that he was much bigger, and his long, muscular body was finished off with a tail of moderate length, which he carried low, with a slight upward lift at the tip.

Micah was simply swept away by the vision, and many of the people on the dock were drawn to the sight and stood near the bottom of the loading ramp to fully appreciate the animal up close.

"Ladies and gentlemen," Colonel Burke proudly announced to the onlookers, "this is a collie, a herding dog originating in Scotland and admired by the late Queen Victoria herself, who brought the noble breed to the world's attention. His name is Pride. Champion Source of Southern Pride, to be specific, and he will be the foundation of what I expect to be many other champion dogs from my kennel."

There was an audible sigh of appreciation from the small crowd as they admired the beauty on display before them.

After a moment during which Pride appeared to be a king

granting audience to his subjects, the dog started to take a step forward.

"Bates!" Colonel Burke cried out. "Catch him, you idiot!"

Bates was standing inside the freight car, well behind the collie, neglecting his responsibility as he shared a cigarette with the clerk. He jumped forward in response to his employer's call, but by the time he reacted, Pride was halfway down the loading ramp.

Responding to the urgency in the Colonel's voice, Micah rushed forward, yanking a thin rope from his waist that he kept on hand to assist in moving freight, and quickly looped it around the dog's neck. He had taken the action without any second thought, and as he came in contact with the dog, he was astonished at the softness of the animal's coat and immediately worried that he may have stepped above his station without permission.

The dog responded immediately, stopped and turned his majestic head to lightly sniff Micah's face, and the boy softly stroked the fur about his head.

"Good work, boy!" Colonel Burke called out with relief. "Fast thinking."

"Give me that rope!" demanded Bates angrily as he rushed toward Micah.

"Hold on there, Bates!" the Colonel yelled, then turned his attention back to the boy and dog.

"Why, I think Pride likes you, boy," he said.

The dog slowly wagged his tail as he continued to lick Micah's face.

"Bring him down here to me," Colonel Burke called out to him.

Micah obliged, and without requiring any coaxing, Pride

walked beside him while Bates, a deep frown clouding his face, observed.

"By God! You seem to have a nat'ral talent for handlin' dogs," the Colonel remarked. "You been 'round many, boy?"

"Not many, sir," Micah replied with a shrug. "He just seems kinda … I don't know, natural, I guess."

"Excuse me, sir," said a thirtyish man in a three-piece suit and bowler hat who had been standing nearby, addressing the Colonel and holding out a hand. "Name's Parker. Raymond Parker. I'd be interested in purchasing a dog of this breed."

"Colonel Grayson Burke," the Colonel said, shaking his hand. "Pleased to meet you, sir. Well, I'm afraid this is the only specimen of this breed in my possession at the moment, so I'm sorry I can't help you right now. A year or two down the road, when I've found a suitable bitch, I'd be right glad to do business with you."

"Ah, too bad," said Parker with a pout. "I'm on my way to Tupelo with my family right now. We'll only be there a few weeks before we move on to Saint Louis. Business, you see. But I'd sure like to get my hands on a dog like that for my youngsters over there before they get too old to appreciate one, and with Christmas almost here and all. Let me ask you, though, sir. Can one expect to pay a reasonable price for such an animal?"

The Colonel acknowledged the man's wife and young son and daughter with a nod and a tip of his hat as he chuckled and patted the man on the shoulder.

"You might find a farm collie somewhere if you got the time to look hard enough. But if you're looking for a collie dog with a pedigree like Champion Source of Southern Pride, my friend, you can expect to pay, shall we say, top dollar."

Roy, who had been watching the action nearby, was listening carefully to the conversation between the two gentlemen. The talk of money stirred his interest.

"Hmm, too bad," the man said with regret. "Maybe when we settle down in Saint Louis ... Well, I thank you for your time, sir."

Tapping the brim of his hat, he turned and gathered his family. Suddenly Roy stepped forward.

"Carry your luggage for ya, Mister?" he asked.

"Certainly," the man replied and nodded. "This way. There'll be an automobile awaiting us."

Roy clumsily accumulated several pieces of luggage and hastened behind the family as they made their way to the front of the train station.

Meanwhile, Colonel Burke stood admiring Pride, as Micah continued to smooth the fur on the collie's back, much to the dog's pleasure.

"Your car's ready, Colonel," a tall, dignified black man dressed in livery said after approaching.

"Yes," the Colonel acknowledged as he awakened from his absorption. "Bates, you go ahead and drive the truck back to the plantation. Pride can ride with me in the car. Make sure his kennel is ready for him, and I'll join you there. You can put the leash on before you go."

Bates cast a jealous glance at Micah as he hastily pulled the rope from around Pride's neck and tossed it at the boy's face, then roughly replaced it with a collar and leash.

"Careful, you clumsy fool!" the Colonel chastised him. "You treat this dog with care. You hear me? Look at the boy there. He knows how. Don't ya, boy?"

"Yes sir," Micah replied quietly, avoiding Bates' icy stare.

"Come on, then," the Colonel ordered. "Help me get him to the car."

The driver gathered the suitcases stacked on the dock, and he, Micah and Pride followed behind as Colonel Burke led the way.

After a few steps, the Colonel stopped and impatiently gestured to Micah.

"Here. Let the dog walk next to me, boy," he said. "Always prompt the dog to walk at my side, and you, you hold back just slightly, maybe a couple steps behind. Not right next to me, but close enough to control the dog. Understand?"

"Yes, sir," Micah replied and did his best to comply. Pride tended to want to linger behind with him, but with gentle coaxing, he was persuaded to travel two steps ahead, next to the Colonel.

Passing through the depot building, they crossed the freshly paved area in front where various coaches, horse-drawn and motor-driven, intermingled as they awaited passengers arriving on the Eleven-Fifteen. Micah recognized a shabbily dressed, fourteen-year-old black youth named Isaac squatting in the shade of a flatbed truck, apparently waiting to assist the driver with freight to be picked up at the station. He often earned a small amount when the man needed help picking up shipments destined for the large department store downtown.

He watched with admiration and returned Micah's silent nod of recognition as he walked proudly by with the dog.

Isaac had never attended school, but he'd been persuaded by Micah's mother to occasionally drop by the house for reading classes, lessons for which she never expected compensation, especially from Isaac. He lived by himself in a lean-to in a wooded area near Micah's house, and she would often invite him to stay for dinner after his lesson. She knew he likely had little to eat other than the meals she shared with him.

Standing to get a better view of Micah and the dog as they walked past him, he was distracted by the sight of Roy as he placed the luggage on the bed of a small truck nearby while a man held open the door of a car for his family to board. Isaac couldn't help his curiosity. It wasn't often he witnessed Roy doing any actual work, and on this particular occasion, he even seemed to be performing his task with enthusiasm.

"Say, Mister Parker," Isaac heard Roy call out as he saw him rush over to the man, "I couldn't help but hear you say you were lookin' to buy one o' them dogs there."

"You mean, the collie?" Parker responded.

"Yeah, that kind," Roy confirmed with a foolish laugh. "You know, sir, workin' down here at the train depot like I do, I seen most ever kind o' dog you can think of. They's people comin' through here with 'em most ever' day, an' I was thinkin' ..."

Roy paused to figure out how to phrase his proposition.

"Yes? Well?" Parker impatiently prompted him.

"See, I might could find somebody might be willin' to sell one o' them dogs like y'all seen. At a reason'ble cost, I mean."

Parker studied the half-witted boy a moment before pulling a business card and a fountain pen from his coat pocket.

"My family and I will be staying at this house on the corner of Glenoak Boulevard and Lynward Drive in Tupelo until Christmas," he said as he swiftly jotted an address on the back of the card. "If you find me a decent collie at a decent price, come see me. There'll be a finder's fee if I'm pleased, especially if you locate one before then."

Roy flashed an oafish grin and nodded his head vigorously.

"Oh, yes sir," he said. "I can garantee a real high-class dog fr ya. You can count on me, sir! Jes' like the one ye just seen over yonder."

Parker gave no response as he pulled the car door shut and his vehicle pulled away.

"I'll be on the lookout! See ya soon!" Roy shouted. He grimaced as he studied the handwriting on the back of the card. He couldn't read.

"Corner o' Glenoak B'lvard and Lynward Draav," he repeated to himself, committing the location to memory as he stuffed the card into his pants pocket.

Isaac watched Roy lazily walk back to the depot. Where, he wondered, would that fool ever get his hands on a dog with the class the man was looking for? While he pondered that question, his attention was directed back to Micah, who stood, still holding the dog near the Colonel's car.

"Mmm-hmm," Isaac murmured to himself, then turned to assist the driver he was working for with a large crate that had been delivered.

Colonel Burke waved aside his driver, who stood with an open door to the rear seating area of a luxurious open-air Cadillac Runabout.

"I'll be driving home, Alexander, the Colonel told him. "Pride can sit up front beside me."

Seating himself on the brightly colored red front seat behind the steering wheel, the Colonel pointed to the opposite side of the car.

"Bring him 'round over here, boy," he instructed Micah,

who promptly complied.

"Now," the Colonel continued, "see if you can't get him to sit up here next to me."

Alexander rushed to assist Micah.

"No, now you just stand back and let me see what the boy can do," the Colonel ordered and Alexander stepped back.

Micah had no way of knowing how obedient the collie would be, but when he looked down into his face, the dog looked back at him, his head slightly cocked, studying his eyes as if waiting for a command.

"Up! Up, boy!" Micah said to him quietly, directing him with a nod of his head to the empty seat next to the Colonel. Pride, who had been panting, closed his mouth and glanced toward the spot he had been directed, then looked back at Micah, as if to confirm the order.

Micah laid the leash across the dog's back and gestured toward the car.

"Go, on!" he ordered. "Git on up there!"

Without further hesitation, Pride obeyed the command and jumped into the seat next to the Colonel, then turned back to face Micah.

"Sit down," Micah said, waving his arm in a downward position. "Sit down!"

Pride sat and continued to look toward the boy for further instruction.

"Well, I'll be damned!" Colonel Burke exclaimed, and sat for a moment, looking at the dog with disbelief.

"What do they call you, boy?" he asked after a few moments.

"Micah, sir" the boy replied.

"How many days they got you workin' down here at the

depot?"

"Much as I can, sir," Micah replied with a shrug. "Weekends and after school a few hours."

"Well, you're workin' for me now, helpin' take care of Pride. Keepin' him exercised, brushin' his coat, cleanin' up the crap he leaves behind. Whatever they been payin' you here, I'll pay you a bit more. Christmas on its way. You'll be needin' some extra cash, I reckon."

Micah could hardly believe what he was hearing. The joy he was feeling was evident in the expression on his face.

"Let's see," the Colonel continued, "tomorrow bein' Sunday, I guess you and your kin will be in church. You be down to my kennels immediately after. You hear, boy? Let's go, Alexander."

His driver stepped in front of the vehicle and laboriously turned the crank as the Colonel started the noisy engine.

"Yes, sir! Thank you, sir," Micah shouted to be heard above the sound of the motor.

Alexander rushed into the back seat and slammed the door shut. Without further word, Colonel Burke shifted the gear and the vehicle slowly started away. As it passed, Micah noticed a look Alexander was casting toward him from the back seat. He seemed to be silently telling him, "You're one lucky boy. Count your blessings, and whatever you do, don't mess this up!"

Suddenly, a thought occurred to Micah that sent his spirits crashing.

How many hours would he have to work? What if it interfered with his schooling? His mother would never, under any circumstance, allow him to miss school. His daddy might not have any strong objection. He'd lecture his son about working hard and saving his money and avoiding confrontation with a white man, but when it came to education, Daddy conceded authority to his wife.

Whatever it would take, Micah was determined to persuade his mother to allow him to work for the Colonel, but as he remained in the parking lot, it was the image on Pride's face, looking back at him while the car sped away that consumed him and left him with an unforgettable memory. As the car faded in the distance, he could still see the collie, sitting straight and strong next to the Colonel, with an expression that seemed to be saying, "I need you, Micah. Please be my friend forever."

The shabby house where Micah lived with his family sat by a tobacco field his sharecropper father tended near a heavily wooded area, two miles from the train depot. He never paid much attention to the meagerness of his living conditions. It was all he'd ever known, and it never occurred to him to want for more.

His father, Jonah, was kneeling in the field among patches of weeds that he was pulling and tossing into a small wagon hitched behind his mule, so consumed by work that he failed to notice his son's return. Though he wouldn't start planting until February, he worked the field every day but Sunday. There was plenty to be done there year-round.

Micah's little sister, eight-year-old Annabel, was drearily sweeping the floor of the small kitchen area when he walked into the house. Annabel's responsibilities on Saturdays included helping their mother, Hannah, with the washing, housecleaning and even the cooking. During the week, Hannah's teaching job at the little schoolhouse afforded her little time to tend to domestic chores, and Saturday was her one day to catch up. Micah found her seated at the kitchen table, snapping green beans into a large bowl, and the tedious, cheerless expression on her face was pushed aside by a bright, broad smile when she saw him.

"What y'all doin' home so early?" she asked cheerfully. "Come give your mama a hug."

His friends would mock him when they saw him gladly accept his mother's hugs, but he was willing to take their ribbing. His mother's embrace always felt so good and warm and comforting, and she smelled of fresh, crisp laundry, recently brought in after hanging in the sun, so let them jeer, he thought. Besides, he knew most of them would be similarly welcomed when they got home, though he was certain no one got better hugs than him.

All the way home he'd debated on the best way to tell his parents about his new job. He tried first to strike up a conversation about the small Christmas tree with its home-made ornaments that stood in the corner of the room. Quickly running out of observations on that subject, however, he decided to just address the matter head-on.

"Momma," he began, "I got some good news."

"Well, good news is always good to hear," she replied, as she resumed her work at the table.

"You know that Colonel Burke, lives on that big farm other side of the church?" he asked.

"There's nobody around here don't know about Colonel Burke. Him and all those dogs of his."

"He's hired me to come work for him, takin' care of one of his dogs. He's gonna pay me more than I been earnin' at the depot."

His mother looked at him out of the side of her eyes.

"How much?"

"I don't know how much yet but, Momma, he wants me to start first thing tomorrow, right after church."

She stopped her work and looked at him directly.

"But Micah, honey, you know we always get together with your daddy's family and my family for early dinner after church. You shouldn't have to work on Sunday. Didn't you tell him that?"

"Well," he said sheepishly, "no ma'am. I didn't think it would be proper to be askin' him right off how much money I'd be making, then demandin' to be let off work early the first day when I haven't even started work yet. He seems mighty, um, what's that word you taught me? Big? Strong?"

"Commanding? Imperious?" she coached him.

"But I will. I'll tell him I got to be done early tomorrow," he replied, nodding.

"Well now, I haven't got time to talk about it right now. I've got to have supper ready soon. You go read a chapter out of 'Treasure Island.' Then go help your daddy finish up outside. We'll talk about this over dinner. Hurry along, now."

Micah had hoped to have his mother thoroughly sold on the new job before breaking the news to his father. He'd be more likely to go along with it if she was already persuaded. If only they could see Pride for themselves. He was certain the sight of the amazing collie would impress them more than any argument he could bring to the table.

It wasn't long before the family had been seated for dinner than Jonah addressed his son.

"So now, what's this I hear about a new job?" he asked.

"Yes sir," Micah replied, stiffening in his seat.

"How much y'all goin' be paid for this new job? What

kinda work y'all goin' be doin'?"

"I don't know how much yet. Colonel Burke wants me to look after his new show dog. Clean his pen, keep him brushed up real good, that kinda thing."

"Hmm," his father said, his brow furrowing into a slight frown. "Colonel Burke. How he come to give the job to you?"

"He's got this new dog. Pride's his name. I got to hold his leash and walk him around a little bit. The Colonel likes the way me and Pride get along. And, Daddy, he's the most beautiful dog you ever laid eyes on. I really want to work this job. I want to work it real bad. I'll keep up on all my schoolwork, and I promise to make it to church and get home in time for dinner with all the folks. I promise."

"That's a lot to promise, Son."

"I know that Daddy, but I can do it. You'll see."

His father chewed on a bit of fat for several minutes as he considered the request.

"What you think, sugar?" he eventually said, addressing his wife.

Hannah shrugged.

"If he thinks he can do it. I've got no reason to complain about the job he's been doin' down at the depot. I guess we got to give him a chance to show us he can do this one."

"And besides," she said looking her husband in the eye, "it might not be too good to get on Colonel Burke's bad side if you know what I'm sayin'. Not with his influence. He might take it kinda personal if a colored boy turned him down."

Jonah stopped eating, and his frown deepened. It took awhile before he spoke again.

"I guess," he finally said, staring down at his plate.

Micah could have cheered.

"Thank you, sir. Thank you! I promise to ... "

"But you be careful now," his father interrupted. "Jes' keep yo head down an' do yo' job. He's got a lot o' white folk workin for him around them dog pens. Don't try to get too friendly with any of 'em. That way can only lead t' trouble, getting' too friendly an' all. Understand?"

There was only one friend Micah wanted in Colonel Burke's kennels, and it wasn't any of the white men.

After dinner and the dishes had been cleaned, Micah and his family gathered on the front porch, as they did each evening at that time. Jonah would sit in a rickety old chair puffing on an old pipe, one foot propped up on a wooden bucket while Hannah sat in her high back rocking chair nursing a cup of coffee. Annabel was seated on one of the wooden steps braiding the hair of a tattered cloth doll while Micah sat one stair higher, idly scratching the step in front of him with the sturdy twig of a tree that, but a day earlier, he had brandished like a pirate sword straight out of "Treasure Island." Now, however, such childish play was far from his mind.

"I wonder how much a dog like Pride costs?" he mused aloud, staring into the twilight beyond the front porch. He was so immersed in his thoughts about the collie, he hadn't even realized he had asked the question aloud until he heard his father respond with a snort and cough on his pipe smoke.

"Son," Jonah said as he pulled his handkerchief from his pocket, rubbing his eyes and nose, "that's not somethin' y'all ever need be worryin' 'bout. You prob'ly ain't never gonna have that kinda money to throw away on no dog. What you think you'd do with it, anyway?"

His father knocked the bowl of his pipe against the porch rail next to his chair.

" 'Sides," he finished, "ain't nobody ever gonna let you walk aroun' with a animal like that, lookin' like you better than ever'body else."

By "nobody," Micah realized his father was referring to white people.

He knew his father loved him, but he sure had a way of crushing cheer underfoot, and now Micah felt a heaviness in the pit of his stomach.

But it didn't stop him from dreaming that night, once he finally drifted off to sleep, of the most beautiful creature in the world.

Micah heard only snippets of Reverend Pike's sermon in the small Methodist church the next morning. He had drifted out of his daydream of the magnificent canine only long enough to catch that the topic covered was derived from Psalm 37:4. The minister elaborated on the question of whether wishing for that which we do not possess is wrong. Micah heard little else, as he stared out one of the tall windows near the pew where he was seated with his family.

It didn't take long for his mother to notice his inattentiveness, and she tapped on his leg with the palm of her hand to signal him back to reality. His father noticed the gesture and cast him a burning glare of reprimand.

"We do not wish for things beyond our reach," the Reverend Lambert preached. "Nor do we base our wishes on other than that which God has ordained for us: our race, our family. For to do so is wrong."

He paused to let his words sink in. They had particular resonance for Micah.

"Be thankful for that what God has given us," he continued, "and learn to use everything we have for His glory and His purpose."

After those words, Micah's thoughts turned inward. He wasn't ready to accept his father's opinion that he could never own a dog like Pride. And what if God wanted him to have one for His glory and His purpose? His internal debate quickly resolved itself in Micah's favor.

That afternoon, he ran the entire three-mile route that led him to Colonel Burke's huge estate, which was located just off the main road. The house, grand and imposing, sat overlooking spacious pastures in which scattered herds of thoroughbred horses were lazily grazing.

There was once much discussion among locals on the topic of the Colonel's title and how he came to earn the rank. There was also a bothersome question as to how his family managed to recover so quickly after the War Between the States. The rumor that endured was that his father had provided secret support to the Yankees, who, in turn, made certain his financial investments were kept secure in a New York bank. After the war, the Burke family and heirs prospered as owners of one of the largest sugar crops in the South. The plantation was one of the few that found no need to resort to sharecroppers but instead managed to farm its lands with paid help, albeit paying them less than a living wage. Young Grayson Burke participated in a couple of the final battles of the war as a fifteen-year-old Confederate soldier, but his duties were carried out in a support capacity, well behind enemy lines, and his father's money was dispersed to the proper authorities to ensure his safety. His rank was earned, not in the Confederate army, but rather in the Northern, where he served as a young officer in the 1870 American Indian wars. Though he returned home with the rank of colonel and a chest full of ribbons, no one was certain exactly what he had done to earn them. In time the fact that he had served a stint in the U.S. Army was forgotten, and he was simply referred to as "The Colonel," a title in that region that was normally bestowed on veteran officers of the Confederate army.

Quickly locating the kennels, Micah sought out Bates, who greeted him icily and with disdain, but he found him less coldhearted than he had expected. Micah figured perhaps the Colonel may have lectured his kennel boss to be wary of being overly spiteful toward him, owing to his special rapport with Pride.

The thirty pens that composed the Colonel's kennels were filled mostly with hunting breeds, all show dogs, all barking and yipping at the outsider. Recognizing Micah's eagerness to join Pride, Bates tormented him by assigning him to clean the kennels and water dishes of all of the dogs except the collie, who was being kept inside a large barn in a specially constructed wire pen amid horse stalls. Two other white kennel workers had been busy at work until Micah was assigned their work. Then they found a nearby bale of hay to sit on while they watched the new hire work. Soon enough, the Colonel swept into the kennel area and chastised them for their sloth, and they rushed to appear busy.

"Bates," he said firmly to his head man, "if you can't supervise the work I'm paying you for, I'll find someone who can. And what's that boy doin' over there? Why isn't he tending to Pride? That's what I hired him for."

"Come with me, boy," Bates snapped.

Micah fell in behind Bates in a flash and was led to the barn, followed by the Colonel.

They found Pride curled up in the far corner of a spacious

wire kennel. Lying on the concrete floor, looking lonely and forlorn, he didn't even raise his head to acknowledge his visitors.

"Wait here," Bates said. "I'll get his leash."

As he scurried away, the Colonel turned to Micah.

"Call him to you, boy."

Micah approached the wire gate and called.

"Pride! Come here, boy."

The dog suddenly lifted his head at the sound of his voice, and Micah was once again amazed at his elegance. The image of the collie he held in his memory after one meeting, exaggerated as that image was, could not do justice to the beauty of the amazing creature who quickly rose to his feet, wagging his tail eagerly as he rushed to greet him at the fence.

"Give the leash to the boy," the Colonel commanded Bates as he returned.

"Take him out, boy," the Colonel told Micah. "Give him a good long walk and a run around the grounds. But no foolin' around, ya hear? This is a mighty important animal I'm entrusting you with here. Don't let him off-leash and don't let him be eatin' any wild animal carcasses you might come across. Understand?"

"Yes, sir," Micah replied breathlessly. "Only, I got to ask you somethin', Colonel. You see, my momma and daddy, they didn't know I'd be comin' down here to work today, and they made me promise to be back home in time for Sunday dinner, and ... "

"You just take Pride for his exercise now," the Colonel said, stopping him with a raised hand. "When you get back, Bates can show you how to brush out his coat. Then you can make sure his kennel is good and clean and then, well, we'll see how fast you can get all that done. Now get along."

"Oh, yes sir! Thank you, sir," Micah said with a smile. He thought he noticed a slight, benevolent smile on the Colonel's face.

Bates handed Micah a leather leash and collar and opened the kennel gate. Micah stepped forward and wrapped the collar around Pride's neck and fastened the buckle securely as the collie lightly licked his hand.

As he walked from the barn with the great dog at his side, he considered that maybe the Colonel was a little different, a little kinder than a lot of the rich old white men he had known.

Maybe, he thought hopefully, the Colonel would sell him one of Pride's pups at a price he could afford. He had some money already saved, and if he worked hard, he might be able to buy one someday. He hadn't forgotten that he had planned to buy his mother a new dress for Christmas, but for now, he preferred not to think about that. Besides, he remembered, she wasn't even aware of his plan, and wouldn't she be just as happy for him if he was able to buy a collie, knowing how much it would mean to her son? For the moment at least, the subterfuge worked for him.

The joy Micah felt in the days ahead was multiplied as he arrived early and stayed late to enthusiastically perform his duties, which he didn't consider work at all. Bates taught him the skills of proper grooming including bathing and brushing and very carefully clipping the fur around his feet and especially around his ears, shaping and sculpting with meticulous precision. No chore was too demanding when it came to tending to Pride, and even Bates had to grudgingly acknowledge that Micah was performing beyond expectation. However, he would never concede that aloud.

The Colonel would often visit the kennels and spent much of the time seated in front of Pride's run, observing Micah as he tended to the show dog, often coaching and offering words of encouragement. Occasionally he would share sandwiches or refreshments brought down from the kitchen. Micah could tell from the expression on Bates' face that such behavior was uncharacteristic of the Colonel, but he knew better than to remark on it.

When the weather was accommodating, the Colonel would even sometimes join Micah and Pride on their daily exercise around the plantation. On those occasions, as Pride walked close to Micah's side, his tail carried high as an expression of pleasure, the Colonel would regale Micah with stories of his exploits as an Indian fighter, and though the boy could tell that the tales were heavily embellished, he said nothing. Micah preferred hearing him tell about dogs he had owned and loved. Those stories often ended in the statement, "But no dog I ever owned seized my fancy like this one we're walkin' with right here." In time, Micah felt a bond with the old man.

When the Colonel was unable to join them, Micah and Pride spent many hours in the fields and woods near the house. The two of them grew close, and Micah even swore the dog could read his mind. He had never been happier.

There was one disquieting occasion, on a late afternoon after school just a few days before Christmas, however, when the Colonel was attending to business elsewhere that Micah dearly wished the Colonel had been with him. Traveling a pathway that led through a heavily wooded area at the edge of the estate, he was enveloped in an uneasy feeling, made all the more acute by a restlessness Pride was exhibiting. The collie's ears were pricked forward as he nervously watched one particularly dense thicket not far from where they were walking, as a consistent, low growl rumbled in his throat.

Micah stopped and watched the area carefully. They were being watched. He could see movement. Pride was shifting about nervously on his leash, sometimes pulling forward, sometimes seeming to want Micah to follow him back to the kennels.

After several anxious minutes, Micah called out.

"Hello?"

At first, his hail was met with silence, but after a moment, a shadowy figure could be seen moving in the brush, and the quiet was broken by a sudden crack as the phantom form stepped on a twig.

Pride responded with a series of ferocious barks as he lunged at the end of his lead, eager to pursue the distant specter that could now be seen running away. One of his lunges was made with such tremendous strength, that Micah's grip on the leash was broken and the collie charged off in the direction of the mysterious trespasser, dragging his leash behind him.

Panicking, Micah desperately ran after him, yelling his name, but the collie would not be stopped as he leaped with formidable speed over the fallen branches and shrubbery, rapidly widening the gap between them. In his eagerness, Micah failed to notice a low-hanging branch that smacked him high on his forehead, swiftly knocking him down on his back.

He could not be certain how long he lay on the ground, dazed and semi-conscious, but as the stars in his vision subsided, he managed to pull himself into a sitting position and paused for a moment to regain his senses. Finally, he realized his predicament, and he moaned in pain as he managed to stand.

The ache in his head was inconsequential compared to the fear that he had lost the dog. The anger he would face from the Colonel was unimaginable, and he was devastated by a crushing feeling of guilt and panic.

Trying to regain a sense of direction, he gradually became aware of the sound of Pride's bark, not far in the distance before him. In a frenzy, he staggered with the best of his ability toward its source. Dizzy but desperate, he quickly reached the collie, whose leash had become entangled in a group of saplings. Pride was fiercely pulling at his unyielding restraint as he continued to bark.

Releasing the leash from its tether, Micah softly spoke words of comfort to the dog, hugging his body close and gradually calming him down. Carefully feeling the dog's body from head to tail, from shoulder to toe, he first assured himself that Pride was unharmed. When he was confident there were no injuries, he was able to regain his breath and composure. The dog had not been hurt, and for that he thanked God.

After resting for a moment, he became aware of an intense pain on his forehead, where he had come in contact with the tree branch, and he noticed that a trickle of blood was traveling from the wound and down his cheek. Simultaneously, Pride noticed the injury and began softly licking his face.

Micah sat on a large, fallen tree to rest and recuperate before heading back to the kennels while Pride lay by his feet, savoring the calming ear rub he was given. As the injury to his head swelled into a sizeable lump, Micah decided not to tell anyone, especially his parents, about his encounter in the woods. He didn't want to give the impression he couldn't take care of himself, and he didn't want anyone thinking his work wasn't safe. After reaching that decision, he summoned the strength to head back.

It didn't take long for Bates to notice the injury.

"What the hell happened to you?" he demanded as Micah lifted Pride onto the grooming table outside his run and began brushing the leaves and twigs from his coat.

"Aw, I guess I wasn't watchin' where I was goin'. Ran into a tree branch."

"Well, that wasn't none too smart, was it?" Bates remarked with a sneer.

On a table nearby, Bates was preparing a dinner of fresh meat and vegetables for Pride and the other dogs. Micah watched him, summoning up the courage to ask him a question he had been trying for several days to find the nerve to ask.

"Mister Bates, sir," he finally spoke. "I been thinkin'. Don't it seem like Pride gets lonely here by himself ever' night? Do you think, I mean, what do you think the Colonel would say if I was to ask him if I could take Pride home with me to my house sometime? Just for one evenin', you understand."

Bates stopped his work and stared at Micah with disbelief.

"Take him home? Who in the name o' hell do you think you are, boy? Listen, you need to know somethin'. You think the Colonel favors you? He just needs you to look after his dog, that's all. His *dog*. You know how important that makes you?"

Bates shook his head and continued his work.

Micah thought long and hard on those words, but in the end, he concluded that they were just words of jealousy.

"Anyway," Micah said, idly kicking a bale of straw, "I'm gonna own a dog like Pride someday, one of my very own. I'll do anything to have one."

"Anything, huh?" Bates responded doubtfully. "I don't think you got the sense God gave a goose! Finish up your work and get the hell outta my sight."

Walking up the narrow road that led to his home, Micah found his father with his head under the water pump in the front yard, his shirt tossed over a bucket nearby while he allowed a heavy stream of water to engulf his head and back. Shaking the water from his hair, he reached for a nearby towel and used it to dry the dampness that remained. Micah held his head low as he greeted his father in passing, but his injury was immediately spotted.

"Wait!" his father said, grabbing Micah by the arm and turning him so he could better inspect his face. "Where'd that come from? You been fightin'?"

"No, sir," Micah replied. "I ... "

His father's face twisted into an angry scowl.

"Someone hit you? One o' the workers over there? The Colonel?"

"No, sir!" Micah exclaimed anxiously. "I wasn't lookin' where I was headed, and I hit my head on a tree branch. That's all. The Colonel, he wouldn't never strike me. Never!"

The screen door slammed behind Hannah, who had overheard the conversation and was now rushing to them as Annabel watched from the porch.

"Here, now," Hannah said, taking charge. "Let me look at the damage." She grabbed the towel from Jonah, dampened it with water from the pump, and began dabbing at Micah's forehead.

"Well," his father considered, "Maybe he didn't strike you, but just th' same, you got to be careful 'round a man like that."

"No, Daddy," Micah said, wincing at the touch of the

towel. "Colonel Burke ain't like that. He ain't."

"He's *not*," his mother corrected him.

"Matter of fact, he's been treatin' me real good," Micah continued. "We go on walks together, and he tells me stuff and he has his people bring me lunch sometimes. He's not like a lot of those other rich men around here. He's a good man, Daddy."

"Listen to me, Son," his father replied. "He may be treatin' you good, lettin' you clean up after his prize dog an' all, but don't go thinkin' he's your friend. 'Cause you go believin' that, you're just settin' yourself up to be hit in the face with the truth, and the truth can sometimes be a big piece a gristle to swallow. Y'all listen to yo' daddy now, Micah. I don't want you gettin' hurt. Y'all got to remember your place, for your own good."

Jonah was about to continue with his advice, but a sharp glance from his wife told him his lecture was finished for now.

"You come on into the house now," Hannah said, gathering up her son and leading him away. "Let's see if we got a salve to put on that sore. Then you can get washed up for supper. Isaac's gonna be joinin' us."

The subject of Micah's injury and his work for the Colonel was not broached again during dinner. The family gathering on the front porch later, after Isaac had expressed his thanks and departed, was a quiet one until Annabel broke the silence.

"Micah? You gonna be gettin' you a dog like Pride someday? Maybe for Christmas?" she asked.

Her brother tossed a small rock he had been toying with at a tree stump in the yard and waited before he replied.

"I'm plannin' to," he finally said. "I been dreamin' 'bout it, anyway."

"You been dreamin', have ya?" his father asked, puffing on his pipe.

"Yes, sir," Micah responded. "Ain't nothin' wrong with dreamin' 'bout somethin', is there?"

"*Isn't* anything wrong," his mother corrected.

"Well now, here's the thing, Son," his father said, clearing his throat. "I guess dreams are somethin' y'all cain't avoid gettin' outta yo' head when you's young, but as ya get older, when you start gettin' to be a man, y'all got to start dealin' with reality. An' sometimes dreams can die real hard."

"I think what your daddy is tryin' to say is ... ," Hannah began.

"Hold on, now," Jonah said, waving his pipe at her. "Don't you be sugar coatin' it."

He pulled his chair closer to Micah, indicating he expected his son to look him in the face.

"When I was about yo' age, I used to dream an' dream. I dreamed I was gonna go to school, get me some learnin' and grow up to be a rich man. Now, yo' mamma, she had a granma was a freed slave, and she taught her how to read and write, an' she got her into school, though it didn't make her rich."

"Oh, just hush up, Jonah," Hannah chimed in. "My education may not have put too many dollar bills in my pocket, but it sure has made me rich in a lot of other ways."

"Maybe if you hadn't married me ... ," Jonah started.

"If I hadn't married you, I wouldn't have had you," she said, pointing at him. "Or you and you," she added, pointing to Micah and Annabel. "I'd say that's worth more than any amount of money can buy."

"The point is," Jonah continued, putting his hand on his son's shoulder, "y'all got to learn to be strong. And dreamin' don't make nobody strong."

Jonah patted Micah on the back and turned to go into the house.

"Get yo'self a good coon dog," he said, as he entered. The screen door slammed shut behind him.

After his father had departed, Micah sat in silence, his eyes on the darkness on the ground, feeling embittered and upset.

"How come he has to make me feel bad like that?" Micah asked his mother.

"Your daddy has had a pretty hard life," his mother said after a while. "I guess he's had a lot of his dreams crushed under the boot heel of reality."

"But Momma," Micah implored, "what kind of life is it without no kind of dreams?"

"*Any* dreams," she corrected. "You know another word for dreams?"

Micah thought hard. "No, ma'am."

"Hope," she replied. "You just keep hopin', and then go right on livin'."

The next day Micah's spirits were lifted as soon as Pride came into view.

"How come he's always so happy to see me?" Micah asked Bates.

Bates shrugged. "You ain't nothin' special. He just knows yer gonna feed him and take him out for exercise. That's what he's happy about."

"I beg to differ, Bates," interjected the Colonel. Micah and Bates hadn't noticed he'd joined them.

Bates nodded his acceptance of the Colonel's opinion and hurried away to tend to other chores.

"Don't believe anything that moron tells you, boy," the

Colonel continued. "If he ever had an idea in that head of his it'd die of loneliness. I believe Pride fell in love with you the very minute he spotted you when he came off that train. You treated him special, and dogs got a peculiar way of judgin' a man's character right off. You don't even have to say nothin' to 'em or feed 'em or nothin'. They just know. That's all. And Pride here, well, this breed of dog is particularly sensitive about things, and they love their families. God, they love a family! See, over the years they learned to take care of flocks of sheep and sometimes, when there aren't any sheep aroun', why, when they spot somebody needs takin' care of, they just move right in and tend to 'em."

"Pride thinks I'm a sheep, sir?" Micah asked as he delicately brushed the dog's coat.

"Oh, I don't know for sure what goes on in that mind of his," the Colonel said with a chuckle, "but he thinks you're somethin' pretty special, I can sure see that."

"I'm gonna have me a dog like Pride," Micah announced. "Real soon."

"How you figure to manage that?" the Colonel asked with disbelief.

"I'll figure out a way," Micah replied, half to himself.

Pride barked and began wagging his tail enthusiastically.

"He's wantin' to go for his exercise," Micah judged.

"Tell you what," the Colonel said with a smile, "You finish brushin' him then meet me out in front of the house. We'll do somethin' a little special today."

Micah's imagination went wild.

"What are we gonna be doin'?"

The Colonel raised a hand to calm Micah's excitement.

"I got some business to take care of in town, and a couple

o' Christmas gifts to pick out, so I figured to take Pride along with me. And, you, too, if you want to be in charge of him."

"Really, sir?" Micah enthused.

"Think how envious all those folks are gonna be in town when they see you walkin' down the street with Pride beside you. I declare, their mouths are gonna drop wide open!"

"Yes, sir, I bet they will, sir!" Micah said with a giggle.

"Alright," the Colonel said as he turned to leave. "I'll go get Alexander to bring the automobile around, and I'll meet you out front soon as you finish up with the brushin'."

Sensing Micah's elation, the collie began barking and moving about the grooming table excitedly.

This confirmed it in Micah's mind. Colonel Burke was a gentleman and a friend.

Leading Pride to the front of the house, Micah found the Colonel's impressive Runabout parked in the driveway, its metal surfaces glistening in the sun and its convertible top down, displaying the luster of its red leather seats. He had never ridden in an automobile so fine.

Colonel Burke was discussing some motoring details with Alexander as Micah and Pride approached. It was apparent that the Colonel intended to drive the motor car himself. His face lit up when Pride came into view, and he rushed to the passenger's side of the car, indicating the front seat.

"Here we go, then," the Colonel said as he stood to the side of the vehicle. "Send him up front with me. 'Atta boy."

Micah started to oblige, then paused, confused.

"What's wrong, boy?" the Colonel asked.

"You want Pride to ride up front with you, sir?" Micah asked.

"Well, yes, of course. What's wrong with that?"

Micah was unsure how to respond. "There's only room enough for two in front. Where am I supposed to ride, then?"

The Colonel looked at him with bewilderment and a touch of irritation.

"Why, in the back seat, of course," he replied with a chuckle. "I'm not gonna make you stand on the runnin' board."

Micah continued to hesitate. A gradual, discomforting realization was starting to settle over him, and it was tearing at his pride. He remembered seeing Alexander relegated to the back seat while Pride rode in front on the day they first met at the train depot. It didn't seem right somehow.

The Colonel eyed him suspiciously, and behind him, Alexander opened his mouth slightly, as if wanting to warn Micah that he was about to tread dangerous waters.

"You don't have a problem ridin' back there, do you boy?" the Colonel asked. All friendliness had vanished from his voice.

"But, sir," Micah replied, his voice much quieter, "how come Pride gets to ride up front and I have to ride in the back seat?"

Alexander, his eyes wide, shook his head at Micah, trying to warn him.

The Colonel eyed the boy with an expression both harsh and disapproving. He glared at Micah for several seconds, as if expecting him to apologize for his boldness. Receiving none, he summoned him toward the car with a slow gesture.

"Bring the dog over here."

Looking downward but maintaining an aura of defiance, Micah obliged.

"Put him in the front seat," the Colonel instructed, the

tenor of his voice careful and commanding.

Micah gave a slight upward tug to Pride's leash and gestured to the front seat with his free hand. Pride looked up at him but did not respond.

"Go on," Micah commanded with a nod, his patience running thin. "Get up there!"

Pride's tail, which he had held high as it wagged when they had approached the car, now dropped low. Dejected, he held his head down. Micah had never commanded him in that tone of voice.

"Go on, I said!" Micah yelled at him angrily as Pride balked.

Impatiently, and rather awkwardly, Micah lifted the collie and placed him in the front seat. Pride sat where he was placed, his head held low.

The Colonel glowered at Micah, then exhaled slowly.

"I think you may have misjudged our relationship, boy," he said at length.

Micah stared angrily at the ground but said nothing.

The Colonel studied him for a moment before commanding him to sit down. Micah sat on the running board, avoiding his eyes.

"Not there," the Colonel corrected. "There!" he said, pointing to the ground.

Micah screwed the courage to look into the Colonel's face and, noting the displeasure expressed there, he reluctantly slid from the running board to the ground.

"Now," the Colonel said as he leaned against the side of his auto. "This is all about me not lettin' you ride in the front seat, is that right?"

Micah gave a slow, sullen nod.

"Well," the Colonel said with controlled exasperation. "You're just a kid, I reckon. You got a lot to learn."

"Kids aren't allowed in the front seat? Is that what you're tellin' me, sir?"

"Kids?" the Colonel asked with disbelief. "No, no, boy. Kids can ride up there if there's room, just not colored kids. You know better than that!"

Micah allowed those words to wash over him before he finally managed to speak again.

"Sorry, sir. I thought you was different from other folks. I guess I was wrong."

"I guess I better educate you, boy," the Colonel said, rubbing his ear impatiently.

"I may have been treatin' you better than other white folks mighta done, but that's just me, I reckon. I just tend to let my softer side cloud my better judgment sometimes. My late wife, Eleanor, she used to chide me 'bout that. So, I don't know, maybe I need to apologize to you for givin' you the wrong impression an' givin' you the idea it was OK for you to step outta your station in life."

Micah stared at the ground. He was used to being treated with disdain, but this time it hurt more than usual.

"See," the Colonel said, struggling for a way to lecture the boy, "your parents should have instilled in you a certain education. They should be teachin' you that you can't go 'round actin' like bein' somethin' other than what you are. Now me, I got no prejudice against your race. Honestly, I don't. But it's just the way things are. Every creature on this earth has got a place in life. You can't help bein' born a Negro boy, and, by golly, if you aren't a proper example of a good one. But, you see, you're still a Negro, and I don't have anything again' you for bein' what you are. You just have to learn to accept it and live with it, that's all. Why, look at Pride there. You think he wants to be somethin' he's not? I think a hell of a lot of that dog, but I'm not forgettin' he's a dog. See, I might throw him some scraps from my dinner table, but I'm not gonna let him sit at that table with me any more than I'd let you do that. Understand?"

Micah understood all right.

"Sir, I don't mean to show you disrespect," he said. "My daddy brung me up to always respect my elders. But, Colonel, sir, you may not let Pride sit at the dinner table with you like you say, but you still let him ride on the front seat, and you don't let me do that."

"Well, I've had enough o' this," the Colonel sputtered, "Just get in the back seat. I'm gonna be late for my appointment."

Micah stood his ground.

"Colonel Burke, sir," he said, looking him in the eye. "I quit."

He cast a parting glance at Pride, who had been watching him with concern throughout the exchange, and turning on his heel, Micah walked away.

The Colonel shouted after him.

"Boy, you got this all wrong. I got nothin' against Negroes. It's got nothin' to do with that. It's just the way things are. How you gonna buy yourself a collie if you haven't got a job?"

"I'll get me one," Micah called back. "I'll find a way."

Later, as Micah walked home, the Colonel passed him, heading to town. He slowed his car to a crawl, keeping pace with Micah, allowing him to see Pride so that he might know what he was missing. Pride whined softly when he saw his friend, and the Colonel, his face flushed with anger, pushed the accelerator to the floor and drove on, leaving Micah in a cloud of dust.

When Micah arrived home he announced to his family that he had quit his job with Colonel Burke. Annabel wanted to know why, but he didn't respond. His parents said nothing as they exchanged worried glances. Hannah followed her son to the tiny room he shared with his sister. He had thrown himself onto his bed and buried his face in his pillow.

"You want to talk about it, honey?" she asked softly.

"No, ma'am," came the muffled reply. "Maybe later."

She patted his back lightly, then turned to go. Pausing at the doorway, she said to him, "It breaks my heart to see you feelin' bad like this, tomorrow being Christmas Eve and all."

When she received no response, she left him, pulling the curtain that hung across the bedroom doorway closed. She chased away Annabel, who was waiting on the other side.

Micah remained in bed, declining to eat dinner and making no acknowledgment of Annabel at bedtime as she climbed onto her side of the small bed they shared and pulled the blanket up high over her shoulders.

He slept fitfully and intermittently throughout the night. Something was bothering him that he couldn't pinpoint, something besides the dispiriting encounter with Colonel Burke. At long last, he finally fell into a fitful sleep just before sunrise. It wasn't for long.

Micah was awakened by a loud banging at the front door. Opening his eyes he could see the first rays of the morning sun illuminating the bedroom as they radiated through his window, and for a moment, the pounding was all that filled his consciousness. Suddenly, he sensed that the urgency with which the door was being beaten must have related to the premonition of ill will that had haunted him the previous evening. He lurched from bed, still dressed in the clothes and shoes he'd been wearing when he came home from work.

Entering the family room of the house, closely followed by Annabel, he found his father, a frightened look on his face, motioning to his mother to stand back as he jumped into his overalls and prepared to open the door.

"Open up!" a man's voice could be heard over the pounding.

Summoning his courage, Jonah prepared to open the door. After confirming that his family was standing back at a safe distance, he cautiously opened the door just enough to show himself. Micah could not see who stood outside.

"I'm Deputy Englehardt," Micah heard the man outside say. "That man over there by the car is Mister Bates. He works for Colonel Burke. Are you Micah Hanes' daddy?"

"Yes, sir," Jonah replied quietly.

Micah could see the deputy's hand as he attempted to push on the door. His father resisted at first, then thinking better of himself, grudgingly allowed the door to be swung wide.

The rising sun shone brightly behind the uniformed deputy who stood framed in the doorway, his eyes squinting to adjust to the dim light inside the house. He held a nightstick in his hand that he had been using to bang on the door. Eventually, his eyes landed, accusingly, on Micah. He motioned to the boy with his index finger.

"Step out here with me for a minute, boy," the deputy commanded.

"What's wrong, deputy?" Jonah asked. "What's happened?"

"Tell your boy to come out here," the deputy replied sternly.

Jonah hesitantly nodded to Micah.

Placing an arm around her son's shoulder, Hannah, still dressed in a threadbare nightshirt, led him toward the door, but she halted by Jonah. The couple held each other tight as Micah went outside.

Micah stared at the ground, afraid to look the deputy in the face.

"Boy," Englehardt said, pointing to his car, "you know that gentleman over there?"

Recognizing Bates, who stood leaning against the deputy's automobile, Micah gave a nod and resumed staring at the ground.

"What?" the deputy said, raising his voice. "Is that a yes?"

"Yes, sir," Micah quietly replied.

"Uh-huh," Englehardt continued, his hands on his hips. "Mister Bates works for Colonel Burke down the road here, and he strongly suspects that y'all stole one of the Colonel's prize dogs."

"What? You mean Pride?" Micah replied with disbelief. He looked up at the deputy with a panic-stricken look on his face. "I never did no such thing!"

"Oh, so you even know which dog got stolen?" the deputy interrupted. "How 'bout we just take a look around then, just to make sure he didn't get loose by hisself and then found his way down here."

The deputy instructed Bates to look around the grounds outside the house while he looked inside. Bates nodded and walked away as Englehardt used the tip of his nightstick to push the door wider. Stepping inside, he halted as he looked around the interior. He moved slowly about, occasionally using his club to lift an object to look underneath. Micah noted his disdainful attitude and his unwillingness to touch anything, using only his nightstick to move objects.

"Don't believe you're gonna find a dog under there, sir," Hannah said as he looked beneath a stack of papers and a book lying on the kitchen table.

Englehardt frowned at her before crossing the floor to enter the parents' room. Hannah rushed to Micah and held him close, and Annabel grabbed her father tightly.

After a prolonged search of the bedroom, the deputy proceeded to the children's room.

Micah wondered why it took him so long to search areas that barely had room to fit one bed. Eventually, Englehardt rejoined them, and Bates called to him from the front door.

"Can't find anything around here," Bates said. "Could be he's hid out there in the woods somewhere."

"I was thinkin' the same thing," the deputy responded in a slow voice. "Or maybe even ... "

He eyed the family suspiciously as he walked out the doorway and down the front porch steps. Micah and his family followed and watched as Englehardt walked along the side of the house before kneeling and bending his head close to the ground to look into the small crawlspace beneath.

After a long pause, he stood and wiped the dust from his hands.

"Mister Bates," Micah said, "You know I wouldn't steal no dog. Not even Pride."

"That's the dog gone missin', didn't you say?" the deputy

asked Bates.

"That's right," came the response. "And the boy said he was gonna get him for his own someday. 'No matter what it takes,' I heard him say and on more than one occasion, too."

"No, Mister Bates, sir, I didn't ... ," Micah tried to say.

"Then yesterday, when the Colonel fired him," Bates interrupted, "I reckon he was so upset about not gettin' to see the dog no more, he figured to get him for himself."

"The Colonel never ... ," Micah began.

"Sir," Jonah said loudly to the deputy. "He told you he never stole no dog. We woulda seen him with it if'n he did, and we didn't see nothin'. I swear to you. Now, y'all didn't find no dog aroun' here, so it's just my son's word again' this man. How come you believe him an' not Micah?"

Englehardt stared at him in disbelief.

"You really don't know the answer to that question?" the deputy asked, glowering at him. "You sure as hell got a God-awful uppity disposition', ain't you? You know, when we find that dog around here, you could be spendin' time in the jailhouse for aidin' and abettin'. Now, I'll just be takin' the boy along with me while we keep lookin' around for ... "

"My boy isn't going anywhere!" Hannah said, holding Micah protectively.

"Aw, now come on," the deputy said with exasperation. "We're just gonna take him down to the jail while we ask him some questions. Don't make this any harder than it has to be."

"Besides," he continued conspiratorially, "when word gets out around town that a little colored boy stole the Colonel's big, pretty dog, well, people might take matters into their own hands like they often do, and I don't have to tell ya how sometimes that can turn out. He'll be safer with the sheriff."

"You know damn well the sheriff won't do nothin' to protect him," Jonah said angrily. "Not any more than he's protected any o' the other colored folks been arrested and lynched 'fore they even had a trial."

Hannah gasped and placed her hands on Micah's ears.

"Jonah!" she exclaimed.

Englehardt pointed his nightstick at Jonah's face, but couldn't find words to dispute him. Lowering his stick, he motioned for Micah to come with him.

"Come on, boy," he said. "Ain't nobody gonna hurt you. It's Christmas time."

"I'm goin' with him," Hannah said.

"You ain't even got any clothes on, schoolteacher!" Englehardt laughed. "Just send him on with me. You can come down to the jailhouse later and bring him some lunch."

Micah grabbed his mother's arm. He knew he had to be strong for her.

"I'll be OK, Momma," he said to her. "I'll see you later. Truth will tell. Ain't that what you always tell me?"

After a moment of consideration, she relaxed her hold on Micah.

"Listen, honey," she said as she knelt and looked her son in the face. "You cooperate with these men, you hear? Don't make them angry, and whatever you do, be sure you tell the truth. Always. You hear me?"

"Always," Micah assured her.

"I'm going to see that Colonel Burke," she added, wiping tears from her cheek. "You said yourself he's been good to you in the past, and maybe ... "

"No, don't go botherin' the Colonel," Bates interjected. "He won't want to get involved with this. Just wait until the sheriff finds out what he needs to know."

"Come on," the deputy said with finality. "Let's go."

He nudged Micah with his stick and motioned for him to crank the car. He tried to oblige but didn't quite have the strength to get the car started. Jonah stepped forward and grabbed the handle and with one crank, the engine chugged to a start. The deputy tossed his head over his shoulder indicating for Micah to climb into the back seat.

During the drive to town, Bates and Englehardt puffed on cigarettes in the front seat, and swapped fishing stories. Micah, meanwhile, gave no thought to any penalty he might be facing. His only worry was for Pride's safety, and he wondered who could have stolen him. He couldn't help but consider that Bates himself might have been responsible.

There were only two cells in the jailhouse, and since a white man was sleeping off a night of drunk and disorderly conduct in one of them, Micah was shoved into the other. He seated himself on the stained, putrid-smelling cot and waited.

In less than two hours, Colonel Burke, followed by Hannah, strode through the door into the small outer office and stood imposingly before Englehardt, who was seated at his desk. The deputy was sipping from a metal coffee cup whose contents smelled of something stronger than coffee, and he was sharing a joke with Bates, who was seated before the desk, unaware that the Colonel had entered the room. Startled at the Colonel's commanding appearance, Englehardt choked on his beverage and assumed a position of attention in his chair.

"I want to see the sheriff immediately!" the Colonel commanded.

Alarmed, Bates nearly spilled the liquid in his cup as he awkwardly set it down and stood beside his chair, visibly shaken at his employer's sudden appearance.

"Well, Colonel," Englehardt said with a quiver in his voice, "this is the sheriff's day off. I'm in charge here right now."

"All right then, deputy, release the colored boy you arrested this morning," the Colonel ordered. "Immediately!" Then he turned and addressed Bates.

"Why didn't you tell me my dog was stolen?"

"Colonel," Bates began, clearing his throat and attempting to gain control of his anxiety, "I noticed the dog was missing early this mornin'. I was hopin' to recover him before you found out, figurin' to spare you the aggravation."

"What proof you got that the boy took him?" the Colonel asked.

"Well, Colonel Burke, sir, he's been sayin' all week he was gonna ... "

"Yes, yes. He wanted a collie of his own to keep. Did he have the dog?"

"No, sir, we haven't found him yet, but ... ," the deputy stammered.

"I thought I told you to release the boy!" the Colonel bellowed.

Englehardt was unable to muster any semblance of authority, and he trembled in the presence of the Colonel's commanding demeanor. Swiftly grabbing a ring of keys, he unlocked the door leading to the jail cells and entered.

"Why didn't you hear the other dogs barkin' last night, if somebody was around the kennel?" the Colonel asked Bates. "Your shack is right by there. Or were you too drunk to hear anything?"

The guilty look on Bates' face answered the question.

"You've been jealous of that boy since he '... ," the Colonel started to say.

"Now just hold on there, sir," Bates said defensively. "I know full well the boy couldn't keep Pride, but I figured he was plannin' to sell him so he could get the money to buy his own collie. It makes sense, don't it?"

The Colonel considered the idea and glanced at Hannah, who stood behind him with her arms crossed. The expression on her face seemed to dare the Colonel to back down.

"Well," the Colonel replied sheepishly.

The door opened, and Micah rushed toward his mother.

"Momma!" Micah cried as he embraced her.

"Colonel, I'm releasin' this boy into your custody," Englehardt said as he returned to his desk. "You willing to take responsibility for him?"

The Colonel nodded reluctantly.

" 'Cause you know how folks are feelin' around town right now," the deputy added. "With the colored situation, I mean. Wouldn't take much to set 'em off, and it wouldn't much matter if a suspect was even guilty."

The Colonel regained his imposing stature.

"You just find my dog," he ordered. Then turning to Bates he commanded, "And you stick around and help him out. Your future as my employee might hinge on your ability to retrieve him. Understand me?"

The Colonel turned to leave, followed by Hannah and Micah. As they left the office, Englehardt called after them.

"Merry Christmas, Colonel Burke!" he said.

The Colonel did not acknowledge him.

Outside, Alexander was standing beside the Colonel's car. Hannah and Micah walked past.

"Hold on there," the Colonel called after them. "I'll give you a ride back to your place."

"We'll manage," Hannah said as they continued to walk.

The Colonel grumbled under his breath as he climbed in and slammed the car door.

On their walk home, Hannah explained to her son why his father had not come with her to get him out of jail.

"I just plain wouldn't let him," she explained. "You know how fired up he can get. He'd have gone down to that jail and raised such a fuss he'd be sittin' next to you behind those bars!"

Suddenly she knelt and embraced him.

"I'm so proud of you, son!" she declared. "You've been so brave. You're my hero."

"Momma, I've got to find him," he told her.

"What? That dog? Nonsense," she dismissed him. "You just let the deputy find him."

"But what if he doesn't?" Micah asked. "Pride needs me. I've *got* to find him!"

It was the only thought on his mind as they continued their walk home.

Arriving at their house, Micah noticed a lone figure standing at the edge of the woods. It was Isaac. He was watching them approach and he waited until Hannah's attention was directed toward Jonah and Annabel, who came running from the house to greet them, anxious to find out what had happened at the jail. When the three of them were not likely to notice, Isaac motioned for Micah to join him, but Jonah grabbed him with a firm hug and tried to pull him inside.

"Daddy," Micah said, pulling back from his father slightly. "Is it OK with you if I just walk around a bit? You know, kind of shake off the bugs from that old jail 'fore I go into the house? I'd feel a lot better if I could." While Jonah was considering his request, he noticed Isaac.

"Sure thing, Son," he replied. "Y'all go tell Isaac what's been happenin'. Maybe you'll feel better."

"Then you come right back here and get into the bathtub and scrub yourself good," his mother added. "You probably got lice from that place. I'll get a bath ready for you. We got a big Christmas Eve celebration tonight, don't forget!"

"Yes, Ma'am," Micah replied and hastened toward Isaac.

The two met, and together they walked the path leading into the woods.

"I been workin' in town this mornin'," Isaac told him. "I heard what happened. They treat you all right at that jail?"

"Yeah, I guess," Micah replied with a shrug. "I wish they hadn't took me there."

"I got kinda worried," Isaac said. "Y'all know some o' them people in town. They all had figured you was guilty 'fore they even heard the whole story."

"They let me go while they try to find Pride. I sure hope they find him soon. I'm worried about him."

"Y'all need to be worryin' 'bout yo'self, Micah! 'Specially since they ain't gonna find him. I know that for a fact."

Micah stopped him.

"How are you so sure?" Micah asked anxiously.

"I'll tell ya how," Isaac replied. "I know who stole him and I also know where he is right now."

"You know that?" Micah yelled, grabbing the front of Isaac's shirt. "Who took him? Where's Pride?"

"Boy, I don't wanna get involved in any o' that," Isaac told him. "I was gonna try to tell the Colonel, but if I tell anybody, they just as likely to blame it all on me. I can hear 'em now:

'How come you to know where that dog is, colored boy? You steal him yo'self?' That's the way it works, Micah. I ain't lyin' to ya."

Micah couldn't grasp Isaac's reasoning.

"But why would they blame you?"

" 'Cause the one who stole him is white, that's why!"

Micah stood silent for a moment, considering Isaac's predicament.

"Who stole him then, Isaac? I got to know."

"I'll tell ya who. It was that blockhead fool, Roy, that's who. I knew he was gonna do it the day that dog came to town. I seen him hidin' 'round in the woods by the Colonel's place, watchin ever'body's comin's and goin's, tryin' to figger the best time to steal that dog."

"Roy? I saw him at the jailhouse this mornin'," Micah remembered. "I wasn't in there too long, but he came in while I was there."

"He come there to see you?" Isaac asked, eyeing him suspiciously.

"Well," Micah replied, "if he did, it was just to treat me bad. He said some awful things at me. I think he was really there to see the deputy. 'Fore he left, he gave him a Christmas present."

"What kinda Christmas present?"

"I don't know," Micah said with a shrug. "He just handed Deputy Englehardt some kinda envelope and said, 'Merry Christmas.' But never mind all that. Where's Pride now?"

"He sold him to some man he was carryin' bags for down at the depot the day that dog got here," Isaac told him. "Roy waited 'til the time was right, then he snuck in, stole him and took him away and sold him. I been watchin' him, and I seen him last night sneakin' with the dog down to the tracks. He caught him a freight car headed outta town, and him and that dog is gone, I tell ya!"

Micah was becoming increasingly distressed.

"If Roy took him off, how you know where Pride is now?"

" 'Cause I heard that man say if Roy could get him a dog like that one 'fore Christmas he'd buy it off him. Said he'd be stayin' over in Tupelo. House on the corner Glenoak and Lynward. Yo' mama been havin' me work on my memory when she teaches me, so I been practicin' and I can 'member pretty good now."

Micah looked at his friend wide-eyed, then turned and started to run back to his home.

"Wait! Wait! Wait!" Isaac yelled after him, and Micah stopped. "Where y'all think you goin'? You gonna tell 'em where he is?"

"Well, yeah," Micah said, panting. "Why shouldn't I?"

"Cain't you figger out what happened?" Isaac asked, walking fast to close the distance between the two of them. "That weren't no Christmas present Roy give Englehardt. He paid him off, and he won't go over to Tupelo t' get that dog. He'll just cover for ol' Roy and claim you musta sold the dog to somebody. Roy's got this whole thing figgered out. He ain't got the brains God gave a pile o' rocks, but when he paid off that deputy, he sure as hell had a plan for this. Those white folks in town? They'll slap you to sleep, then slap you for sleepin'!"

Micah started pacing in circles.

"Then, I got to get him back myself," he concluded. "I'll go get him and sneak him into the kennel without anybody seein'. Once he's back, there won't be any problem."

"Aww, Micah," Isaac exclaimed with exasperation. "I knew you'd try to do somethin' stupid like that. What was I thinkin', tellin' you 'bout all this?"

Micah squinted.

"Yeah. Come to think, why'd you tell me?"

" 'Cause," Isaac said with a heavy sigh, "I guess ... "

He started to laugh.

" 'Cause I knew you'd try to do somethin' stupid like that, and I figgered I'd help ya, I guess."

Micah laughed too.

"You already got a plan?" he asked.

"I'm just gonna go down there, steal that dog back and sneak him into Colonel Burke's kennel, that's all," Isaac answered.

"OK," Micah said, "but I'm goin' with you."

The two of them argued the issue for several minutes until Isaac, with a lengthy sigh, gave in to Micah's insistence.

"Yeah, I figgered you'd insist on that, too," Isaac said. "You gonna have to sneak out be here by ten-thirty tonight if we gonna catch that freighter to Tupelo. Your momma been teachin' me to read maps, too, so I know right where to go to find that dog. But we're gonna have to act quick so we can catch the freighter in time comin' back. I figger we should be able to get home 'fore daybreak 'less we run into trouble, which sho' could happen!"

"There ain't gonna be any problem, Isaac," Micah assured him.

"Uh-huh," Isaac responded, unconvinced.

Nightfall couldn't come soon enough to suit Micah, and all the Christmas Eve activities in which his family traditionally participated seemed to last longer than he could remember their lasting before. After his bath, there was a brief service at the church, a hearty dinner at home, which his parents insisted he finish completely, followed by a gathering around the fireplace to tell ghost stories and sing carols.

Micah's impatience did not go unnoticed by his parents and even Annabel exclaimed, "What's troublin' you, Micah? You anxious for Christmas day to get here?"

He barely heard her words. His mind was filled with excitement and anticipation, and the hours just seemed to be dragging by, indifferent to his restlessness. He knew he would have to sneak out of the house not later than ten-fifteen to meet Isaac in time to catch the train. By nine o'clock, dressed for bedtime and ready to burst, he managed to restrain his nervousness as his mother read from the Gospel of Luke to the family. Then it was bedtime, and after goodnight kisses and after all the lamps in the house were extinguished, the curtain was drawn across the children's doorway, and the evening finally came to an end.

It didn't take Annabel long to fall asleep, but Micah grew more distressed as he heard the muffled sound of his mother and father talking quietly amongst themselves in their bedroom. He was worried they would still be awake when it was time for him to sneak out of the house. Their discussion carried on for some time, and it wasn't until a few minutes before ten o'clock that their conversation ended. He was relieved to hear the sound of his father's snoring shortly after that.

When he felt it was safe, Micah cautiously stepped out of bed and slipped into the clothes he had secretly placed beneath it. The only window in the room was slightly ajar to allow for fresh air, but behind the window sat a screen mesh, and fearing that its removal might make enough noise to waken Annabel, if not his parents, he opted instead to steal quietly out the front door. If he was overheard passing through that way, he hoped his parents would assume he was just taking a trip to the outhouse.

The main room of the house was darker than usual, mainly due to the Christmas tree that had been placed before the front window. Though the tree was sparsely decorated, its branches prevented little light from entering the room on a wintery night when the sky was already heavy with clouds. The embers still burning in the fireplace cast just enough light to allow Micah to make out his father's badly tarnished old pocket watch that he always left each night sitting next to his pipe on a small table by the overstuffed chair that faced the hearthside. Holding up the watch, he could barely make out that the time was exactly ten-fifteen. He put the watch in his pocket.

Moving stealthily across the room, he ever so slowly opened the door and screen door, neither of which was locked, nor were they equipped with springs of any kind. Micah prayed that the creaking sound made by the hinges would not waken anyone, and he paused a moment to ensure he had not been heard before carefully closing the door behind him. He was grateful for his father's snoring, which drowned out the groaning of the hinges. Noiselessly crossing the front porch, he was off.

He could make out the faint figure of Isaac, waiting for him at the edge of the woods.

"We got to hurry!" Isaac said to him in a loud whisper, and the two friends rushed into the night, following a barely visible path through the woods that would lead them to the train tracks.

The short hike delivered them just in time to meet the freight train that would deliver them to their destination. The freighter regularly slowed at this point before picking up speed for the last leg to Tupelo, and it didn't take long for the boys to find an empty car that wasn't already occupied by hoboes. After a quick run and an energetic jump, they were on board a paneled car whose side door had been left open.

"Y'all got to be careful which one o' these things you pick out," Isaac said, breathing heavily as he settled in. "Y'all don't wanna get on no cattle car, even when they ain't no cows on board. Let me tell you, them cars stink! Whoo hoo!"

Micah laughed as his breath caught up with him.

"Now," Isaac told him, moving closer to emphasize his point, "I'm lettin' you go wit' me, but only on one condition. You hear me?"

Micah nodded.

"You got to swear to me," Isaac continued, "*swear* to me that no matter what, if somethin' happens to me, you high tail it home without lookin' back. *No matter what.* You promise me?"

"But Isaac ... ," Micah began.

"No, now you listen," Isaac interrupted angrily, "you do what I say. If I get caught, you just keep on runnin' 'til you cain't run no more. It don't make sense both of us gettin' throwed in jail. You promise you do that or I'm gonna throw you right off this train right now."

Micah hesitated, and Isaac grabbed his arm and squeezed it tight.

"Y'all got to promise me, Micah," Isaac shouted. "Yo' momma won't never f'give me if you was to get caught. I don't care about you, but she been so good to me, this ain't no kinda

Christmas present for me to be givin' her. Now, you gonna promise me or what?"

Micah nodded reluctantly and Isaac relaxed.

"Fact is," he continued, "*I* wouldn't f'give myself neither."

The train picked up considerable speed as it distanced itself from the outskirts of the little town, and Micah's heart raced as he peered out the open doorway of the freight car at the dimly seen objects zooming past. He focused his mind on Pride and the mission he had assigned himself and tried to ignore the nervousness Isaac was unsuccessfully trying to hide.

The hour's journey passed quickly, and soon the huge, loud, lumbering freight train was noisily decreasing its speed as it reached the outskirts of the big city.

Gathering himself, Isaac pulled a badly worn piece of paper from his shirt pocket and unfolded it on the floor of the freight car. Removing a matchbox from his pants pocket, he struck a match and used the brief light to study what Micah could now clearly see was a street map. Looking out the door at a tall building situated near a road the train crossed over, he carefully located its position on the map. He gradually assumed an expression of confidence.

"Yeah," he confirmed. "We're nearly there."

Isaac moved to the doorway and sat with his feet dangling outside. He motioned for Micah to join him and instructed him to prepare to jump.

"Them bushes!" Isaac said excitedly. "Just before the road. When I say, y'all *jump*. OK?"

Micah acknowledged the instruction and prepared himself, but as he moved into place, his right hand, which aided him in balancing on the ledge of the doorway, slipped. Losing his balance, he fell forward and, unable to regain a counterbalance, fell free of the car to the hard ground beside the tracks.

"No! Not yet!" Isaac hollered. Given no choice, he swore under his breath and jumped after Micah. Distracted, he failed to notice a power pole the train was about to pass, and his body slammed against it with considerable force, knocking the wind from his lungs as he subsequently fell to the ground.

Micah had rolled rapidly as he hit the hard dirt, but other than a few scrapes and bruises, was relatively unharmed. Shaking his head, his focus fell on Isaac, who lay motionless and face down at the foot of the power pole he had hit. Yelling his name, Micah rushed to him as the train's caboose rolled by.

"Wake up, Isaac! Wake up!" Micah called to his friend as he tried to roll him over. "You okay?"

Isaac groaned, and his eyelids fluttered as he attempted to regain his senses. His breath had been knocked from him, and he was finding it difficult to get it back, but he managed to reply with a barely audible, "Yeah."

Suddenly realizing the urgency of their mission, Isaac tried to sit upright, but an intense pain shot through his back and he reacted with a loud wail.

"Mah back!" he managed to gasp. "I think I broke it!"

"You think you can walk?" Micah asked tremulously. "You think you can get up?"

Isaac remained seated for a few minutes, breathing heavily. Finally, inhaling deeply, he wrapped his arms around the power pole, and with a painful heave, he managed to stand, leaning against the pole and breathing laboriously as he winced with pain.

"What we gonna do now?" Micah asked fearfully. "You ain't gonna be able t' walk like you are."

Isaac shook his head. Looking around, he nodded toward a nearby oak tree.

"Grab a heavy branch off'n that tree over yonder," he managed to gasp as he pulled a pocketknife from his pocket and handed it to Micah. "Pull off the leaves. Make it so I can use it like a crutch."

Micah did as he was asked and managed to find a strong branch that he broke into a six-foot length before chopping off the smaller branches and leaves affixed to it. He offered it along with the knife to Isaac, who clutched the makeshift staff with both hands and used it to stand independently of the power pole.

Gathering his strength, Isaac took a few tenuous steps, relying heavily on the makeshift crutch.

"Alright," he said, puffing as he paused. "You gonna have to help me along, Micah, but we can make it if we get movin' now. You ready?"

"If you think you are," Micah said, nodding.

"Alright then," Isaac said, as Micah placed his arm around his waist and helped move him, staggering and cringing with pain. It was a considerable burden for the younger boy to manage, but he was determined to complete their task and get Pride back home.

When they had traveled about a block, Isaac motioned for Micah to sit him down on a small brick wall that surrounded a large house on the corner. Pulling the wrinkled map from his pocket, he studied it a moment before pointing down the street to his right.

"This way," he said. "Two blocks. We doin' good."

It didn't seem to Micah that they had been successful up to this point, but he assumed Isaac was just trying to be optimistic. They had lost valuable time having to move so slowly, and they would continue to lose time on the return trip. Getting back to the railroad would be tight, and they didn't even know what obstacles would be in their way once they reached their destination.

Holding his breath, Isaac pulled himself to his feet with a slight whimper and an assist from Micah, and they resumed their trek.

With Isaac's handicap, the two blocks they walked might just as well have been two miles. There were few people on the streets except for the occasional pedestrian, usually fairly inebriated, staggering home under the electric street lamps after attending an elegant Christmas Eve party at one of the large, expensive houses in the district. Only a couple of cars and one horse and buggy passed by before they reached an area where a residential street emptied into a large park on their left. A house rested on the corner where they halted, and Isaac nodded to an impressive three-story residence situated on the opposite corner. The house was festooned with wreaths and elaborate garlands to which many colorful Christmas decorations were attached.

"That's got to be the place," he said.

Micah was amazed at Isaac's uncanny ability to deduce which house might be the right one until he noticed the "For Sale" sign on the gate of the house on the corner where they stood. It appeared to be empty.

Placing his finger to his lips, Isaac tossed his head as a signal for Micah to follow him to the house across the street. The front yard was surrounded by a six-foot wrought-iron fence, and the backyard was enclosed within an eight-foot brick wall, upon which a few bare vines clung tightly. An alleyway ran behind the backyard fence, separating the property from the residence behind it. Casting furtive glances to make sure they were not being observed, the two adventurers entered the alleyway and paused in a darkened area at the back wall.

"I sure hate to hav'ta say this," Isaac said, leaning against the wall for support, "but y'all gonna have to do this on your own. I cain't climb over this fence, and I don't think it's a good idea to try to break into the house through the front, so you're gonna hafta see if you can get in through the back."

"I can do that," Micah proudly proclaimed, rising to his full height.

Isaac studied the wall for a minute, then appraised Micah's stature, which was just short of five feet. Arriving at a plan, he leaned his makeshift staff against the wall.

"Here's what we goin' do," Isaac announced. "Y'all use this stick to help you climb up as far as you can get, and use me to support yo'self. Then when you high enough, reach up there an' grab ahold o' that big thick vine up there. See which one I mean?"

"Isaac, I'll hurt your back if I grab hol' of it," Micah said.

"Y'all don't worry 'bout that," Isaac replied. "Let me worry 'bout it. Here. Take this."

Isaac handed him his pocketknife. Micah stared at it in disbelief.

"You 'spect me to use this?" he asked.

"Y'all be needin' something to jimmy the lock on th' door, don't ya?" Isaac asked with an air of exasperation. "An' what if the dog's tied up? Now come on, get goin'. We got to find that dog an' get outta here quick."

There was no time to argue. Micah stuck the pocketknife

in his pants and placed a foot high on the staff that leaned against the wall as he grabbed the top of Isaac's shoulders. Counting to three, he boosted himself up, leaning heavily against Isaac for support. His friend stifled a scream of pain as Micah placed pressure against him.

"You alright?" Micah asked.

"Y'all don't be worryin' 'bout me," Isaac grunted angrily. "Just hurry up an' get off my damn back!"

Micah reached for the vine that embraced the wall. It traveled up and over the the top and would make an excellent way to complete his climb, but to get himself lined up with it, he knew he'd need to give himself a boost up by shoving off Isaac's shoulders with his feet.

"Hold on, Isaac," he said. "This is gonna hurt."

"Just get yo'self over the damn wall, boy!" Isaac managed to gasp.

With no hesitation, Micah shoved off from Isaac's shoulders, pushing him to the ground, where he did his best to squelch a scream of pain. The boost enabled Micah to reach the vine, which he clutched tightly with both hands. A portion of it snapped under his weight, momentarily causing him to lose his grip and nearly sending him falling backward. He quickly managed to grasp a higher section, which held.

With two strong pulls, Micah was able to reach the top of the wall, and after additional clambering, he managed to sit astride it. He remained in that position for a moment, peering into the darkness, taking in the details he could make out of the backyard. He was able to make out two trees, several flower beds and some lawn furniture placed at various locations about the yard. A patio cover extended about twenty feet from the back of the house, and its roof cast a dark shadow over everything beneath.

"Micah?" Isaac quietly called up to him.

At the sound of Isaac's voice, Micah became aware of a metallic sound like a chain being dragged along concrete, and he could make out something, very faint in the darkness, moving toward him from under the darkened patio. Within moments, he knew what it was.

Pride's loud, excited bark was unmistakable.

"He's here!" Micah called back to Isaac. "They tied him up. Now, why would they do that to him on Christmas Eve?"

"Aw, hell, Micah," Isaac called back. "Stop talkin' and get the dog! He's wakin' up the whole damn neighborhood!"

Amid Pride's barking, Micah sprang into action. Leaping from the wall, he landed on the grass of the backyard, and without missing a beat, ran straight to the area where Pride was lunging against the chain that restrained him to a pillar which supported the patio roof. Micah knelt next to the collie to examine his fastening as the dog happily jumped all over him, licking his face and barking. Pride's rowdy behavior was making it difficult to figure out how to release him.

Isaac was using his staff to pull himself back up to his feet when a light went on in an upper window at the back of the house on the other side of the alley. A window slid open, and a male voice called out, "Make that damn dog shut up!"

A light went on in an upper window of the house where Micah was working feverishly to release Pride. The glow of the light from the window reflected brightly down on him, and he swiftly pulled the dog back under the patio, so he couldn't be seen. Struggling with the chain, he found that it was tied to a thick rope that surrounded Pride's neck. The rope was too tight to slip over his head, so Micah began trying to loosen the knot that secured the chain as he desperately begged Pride to stop barking and be still.

"That does it!" the man in the back house yelled. "I'm calling for the police!"

"Micah!" Isaac shouted.

As he tried in vain to loosen the knot on Pride's neck, Micah could hear the sound of doors slamming, voices shouting and footsteps descending stairs inside the house. Suddenly remembering, he pulled the pocketknife pants pocket and began cutting at the rope.

In moments, he was able to cut through Pride's binding, and he ran for the wall, with the dog continuing to joyfully jump up on him. Pausing at the wall, Micah was stunned at the height of the barrier. Had it been that high when he had climbed over? How was he to get back over it with Pride?

Turning around, he spotted a wooden lawn table. Despite its considerable weight, he managed to drag it to the wall. He stumbled before reaching his destination and Pride rushed to lick him vigorously in the face before he was able to get back to his feet. He lifted Pride to the table and crawled up beside him.

"Isaac!" he called out. "I'm gonna have to throw him over to you. You got to catch him!"

"What? Are you crazy, boy?" Just the thought of catching the dog gave Isaac the feeling knives were sticking into his back.

"It's the only way," Micah shouted back. "He's comin' over now. Get ready!"

With almost superhuman effort, Micah boosted the dog as high as he could. Pride, fearful of being placed at that height, began clawing at the air with his front feet until he came in contact with the top of the wall. A shove from behind put him on top. He balanced himself there for a moment with all four feet tightly gathered together, his tail held firmly between his rear legs until Micah gave him another shove from behind.

"Here he comes!" Micah exclaimed as he scrambled over the wall after the dog. Boosting himself over, he could hear someone approaching from behind, yelling for him to stop.

Isaac did his best to catch the dog, but the sudden drop into his arms flattened him to the ground. Pride lay on top of him but quickly stood and shook himself before running to Micah, who landed beside him.

Micah knelt beside his friend who lay completely immobile.

"Remember what I told you?" Isaac was able to gasp. "Now get. NOW!"

"Here they come!" the voice yelled from the house in back. "Here comes the police!"

Gritting his teeth, Micah handed Isaac his pocketknife as he stood and wiped a tear from his eye, then called for Pride, and together they rushed out of the alley and into the street. He stopped half a block away to look back and saw a policeman, blowing frantically on a whistle, rushing to the back alley, where he could hear the sound of considerable commotion.

Pulling his father's watch from his pocket, he could barely make out the time through his tear-filled eyes.

"Come on, Pride," Micah said to the collie, and they ran as fast as they could toward the train tracks.

Micah had neglected to bring a leash with him but found one wasn't necessary as Pride ran gleefully by his side, barking happily, his tail held high.

Reaching the railroad, Micah panicked when he saw no train approaching. Had he missed it? Leaning down and placing his ear to a rail, he was relieved to hear rumbling and could feel a vibration that told him the train was approaching. Pride took advantage of Micah's prone position to lick his cheek.

In minutes, the light of the steam locomotive came into view, traveling slowly but picking up speed as it approached. Micah removed his belt and placed it around Pride's neck, pulling him away from the track to await an empty car. Gradually the wagons passed, though much to Micah's frustration, most of them were full, but in time, an empty car, door open, moved by, and he lifted Pride into his arms and rushed to climb aboard as it rolled by.

The train was traveling at a speed just slow enough to allow Micah to shove the reluctant collie aboard. Pride turned to look at him, blocking the area where Micah hoped to lift himself after him.

"Get back! Get back!" he yelled, but Pride didn't understand his command and only stood his ground, barking.

The train began picking up speed at a faster pace, and before Micah could manage to grab the metal loop to pull himself into the car, his foot hit a rock by the track, and he fell to the ground, barely missing the track itself, where he would have been crushed by the train. He quickly stood and was shocked to see Pride looking back at him from the doorway of his car as it began rapidly moving away.

With every ounce of strength he could muster, Micah ran frantically, trying to catch up to Pride's position, but it seemed that with every burst of speed he could produce, the train increased its speed by double, widening the distance between

Micah and the collie. He knew he would be unable to catch up, but quickly realizing another option, he grabbed a handle on the door of the first car that passed him, and though his body was suddenly jerked sideways, he held tight with unyielding endurance as his feet, unable to keep pace, dragged the ground. Managing to clutch the handle with both hands, he was able to reach a horizontal panel of wood above, lifting himself to a better position. He had attached himself to a cattle car, its walls constructed of boards spaced just far enough apart for Micah to clutch and eventually stand on a ledge that ran the length of the car. As he moved, the smell from its interior reminded him of Isaac's warning.

When he felt secure enough, he began edging his way along toward Pride, which he estimated to be about four car lengths ahead. As he moved along, he was suddenly startled by a burst of profanity and racial epithets hurled at him from within the car to which he clung tight.

"This is *my* spot!" the male voice screamed. "Get outta here or I'll knock ya senseless!"

The man inside began beating Micah's fingers with a stick, and he nearly released his grip in pain, but with effort, he was finally able to pull himself along and away from the madman in the cattle car.

Pride continued barking at Micah, and what would have normally been regarded as an annoyance, instead served to hearten him. As he pulled himself along precariously from car to car, he imagined he was hearing the collie calling to him, "Come on, Micah! You can do it! Come on!"

That encouragement was all he needed to reach his destination, and as he arrived at the doorway of Pride's car, he awkwardly pulled one hand away from the handle he was clutching to push the dog back and out of his way so that he could swing his body inside. Once he had accomplished that task, he lay on the floor, panting and gasping for breath as Pride licked his face. Micah could not recall ever having been greeted with such love and gladness.

During the hour-long journey home, Micah's mind was numb from exhaustion and worry. He could not conceive of any scheme to rescue Isaac, and the guilt he felt for leaving him behind was overwhelming.

At long last, the train began slowing its speed, and Micah began trying to determine the best point to disembark that would deliver him closest to Colonel Burke's estate. Pride balked as he wrapped his arms around him and picked him up, watching for the softest spot to toss him. When at last he set on the best location, he hurled the collie as far as he could from the side of the train into an accommodating growth of shrubbery that cushioned his fall. Micah quickly followed behind.

A walk of twenty minutes delivered the boy and the collie to Colonel Burke's kennels. The location of Pride's run inside the barn made it possible for Micah to sneak him in undetected through a doorway distant from the other dogs, who would have created a commotion had they been heard. Slipping Pride into his enclosure, he filled a bowl of water and placed it inside before securely closing the gate. When the collie began eagerly lapping up the water in his bowl, Micah took advantage of the distraction to withdraw, quietly closing the stable door behind him. All of his careful precautions, however, were for naught.

As soon as he began to rush away from the door, Pride discovered his absence and began barking noisily. This caught the attention of the other dogs in the runs nearby, and they joined in the clamor. Micah started to run, and then suddenly stopped.

He had forgotten to remove his belt from Pride's neck! A light was turned on in a small structure near the barn, signaling that Bates was awake. There was no time to hesitate, Micah reasoned. He would have to take a chance that his belt would not be identified, and he ran away from the barn at top speed.

The time spent running to his home went by quickly. His mind was focused on Isaac's plight, and he was oblivious to all else. When at last he wearily approached his house, he did not at first notice the figure seated on the front porch steps until his father's voice greeted him in the darkness.

"Any luck?" Jonah asked.

Momentarily startled, Micah at last relaxed. The sound of his father's smooth voice comforted him and seemed to convey that there was nothing to fear.

"Yes, sir," Micah replied. "We got Pride back. I put him back in his pen."

His father was dressed only in his trousers and a light blanket was draped over his bare shoulders to spare him the night-time chill. Producing his pipe, he casually began lighting it.

"Well, that's a good thing," he said. "I figgered you was out lookin' for him."

Micah could no longer restrain himself, and in a rush he began pouring out the story of his adventure that evening, culminating in Isaac's fate. He hadn't been aware of the tears streaming down his face until his story was told.

His father listened with furrowed brow before pulling Micah down beside him and laying an arm across his shoulders.

"Hmmm," his father mused. "Then I reckon we better see

if they's anything we can do to help young Isaac."

"But, Daddy!" Micah exclaimed. "If you go down there askin' 'bout Isaac, they might think you're the other one got away with the dog. They might lock you up, too! You can't let 'em do that to you. You have to be here to help me an' the family!"

"Well, that's true," his father replied. "But what you did tonight, the brave things you did, you proved you're a man an' I'm real proud o' you. I pert' near think you could take care o' this family OK on your own, even if somethin' should ever happen to me. That's somethin' give me real peace o' mind, Micah. Real peace o' mind."

"Tell you what, Son," he continued as he stood. "Let's get to bed now, 'fore your mamma knows you been gone. No need getting' her upset Christmas mornin' an' all. T'morrah we can think on what we can do 'bout Isaac. Daylight's gonna be here real soon. Come on, now. Off to bed."

His father laughed as they went into the house.

"That dog!" he chuckled. "He shore has stirred things up, I got to say!"

Micah agreed.

Christmas Day at Micah's house traditionally began with a quick breakfast before everyone, clean and bright, piled into the small family wagon and his father's old mule pulled them to church for Christmas services. Then it was back home to exchange what few gifts (usually hand-made) that had been carefully placed under their little tree, followed by a sumptuous Christmas dinner. Throughout the remainder of the day, they would greet friends and relatives who dropped in to share the spirit and (in the case of their father) *spirits* of the season.

On that particular Christmas morning, Micah felt it best

not to immediately tell his mother about the previous evening's exploits. There would be time enough after all the day's festivities. Somehow, however, Micah guessed that his father may have already told her.

"Micah?" Annabel asked as her mother brushed her hair. "Was you out someplace last night? Seems like ever' time I turned over you wasn't there. Was I dreamin' or what?"

Their mother's face turned to stone, and her jaw tightened. After a moment she glanced at their father as he did his best to hide a smile and excused himself to harness the mule. Everyone ignored Annabel's question.

Walking out the door, Jonah swept up his watch, which Micah had thoughtfully returned to its usual resting place on the small table, but as he began winding it, he glanced at the watch's face and paused, examining it quizzically. The glass crystal was scratched and cracked. Saying nothing, he shoved it into his coat pocket and continued outside.

Any doubts as to his mother's knowledge of the previous evening's events were squelched as the family returned home after the Christmas service to find Colonel Burke's car parked in front. He was seated in back, formally dressed, puffing on a cigar with Pride sitting at his side while Alexander stood beside the car in full livery.

Hannah stepped from the wagon and approached the car.

"Good morning, Colonel," she greeted him. "Merry Christmas to you, sir."

A broad smile covered his face as he returned the greeting, tipping his hat. Jonah nodded his response before leading the mule and wagon to the back of the house. Annabel rushed forward to admire the automobile, and Micah stood behind his mother.

Pride began barking as soon as he recognized Micah.

"Shush, Pride," Micah commanded out of habit. "Stop that barking!"

To his surprise, Pride complied, and he sat wagging his tail excitedly. The Colonel laughed.

"You know anything about this?" the Colonel asked Micah as he gestured to the collie.

Hannah glanced down at Micah, who replied sheepishly, "He's back, sir."

"Indeed. Indeed," the Colonel said with amusement. "And I'll wager you know somethin' 'bout how he wound up back in his enclosure last night."

Micah stood silently, uncertain how he should respond.

"By the way," the Colonel continued. "I paid a visit to Deputy Englehardt's office early this mornin' to let him know about the mysterious reappearance of Champion Source of Southern Pride, and while I was there, the deputy had a visitor, a police inspector who drove all the way down here from Tupelo on Christmas Day on behalf of a Mister Parker. That name mean anything to you? Parker?"

"No, sir," Micah responded, uneasy about the direction the conversation was headed.

"No?" the Colonel asked, feigning surprise. "Hmm. Well, it seems this Mister Parker was paid a visit day before yesterday by an employee of our train depot, a fella by the name of Roy. Now that's a name I'm sure you would recognize, your co-worker at the depot?"

"Yes, sir," Micah replied quietly.

"Well," the Colonel continued, "seems this Roy character sold Mister Parker what appeared to be a full-blooded collie dog, and he made this sale on exactly the same day Pride here went missing. You see what that suggests, don't you, boy?"

Micah nodded.

"Now last night," the Colonel said, puffing on his cigar, "last night, it seems two young colored boys snuck over the back yard wall of Mister Parker's residence under the cover of darkness and stole his newly purchased collie. One of the two boys got away with the dog, but the other individual was injured, and he got left behind. They got him in the jail down there in Tupelo. He won't give any information 'bout his co-conspirator, though. Ahh, he'll probably wind up servin' on a chain gang for a few months for breakin' and enterin' or some such charge. Found a knife on him. Well, he'll be alright. Only thing the police can't figure out down there is this: If that boy and his friend knew Roy stole my collie and sold him to Mister Parker, and if they even knew where Mister Parker lived, why didn't they tell our Deputy Englehardt? He could have gone down there and brought my dog right back to me, 'less they was plannin' to re-sell the dog themselves. Only, if that was their plan, why'd Pride wind up back in my kennel?"

"Anybody talk to Roy yet, sir?" Micah asked.

"Tsk," the Colonel mused, "well, after the visit from the inspector, our Deputy Englehardt went out lookin' for young Roy. He reported back to me on the telephone a short while ago. Seems Roy is out of town somewhere. Not sure where. Maybe he's visitin' some relative for Christmas or somethin'. Well, Englehardt promised me he'd get to the bottom of it. I reckon we can trust him."

Even as he spoke those words, the Colonel did not sound convinced of his own statement, and he sat for a moment considering it as he continued to puff on his cigar. Finally, he signaled for Alexander to open his door. The Colonel stepped from his car and the door was promptly closed behind him. Pride rushed to the window seeking Micah's attention.

"May I, sir?" Micah asked, nodding to Pride.

"Certainly," the Colonel responded, beaming as Micah stepped forward and commenced to scratch Pride's neck affectionately.

"Alexander," said the Colonel, nodding to the front seat.

Alexander stepped to the trunk of the vehicle and, opening it, produced a large platter, covered with a silver cloche, which he presented to Jonah.

"Christmas ham," the Colonel said. "Merry Christmas to y'all."

"Colonel Burke, sir," Hannah responded, "you didn't need to do this."

"Course I did," the Colonel chuckled.

"Jonah," Hannah said to her husband, who stood holding the platter with his mouth open, "why don't you take that on into the house?"

Jonah complied as Hannah thanked the Colonel.

"Oh, and I got somethin' for you, too," the Colonel remembered.

Leaning back in the car, he produced Micah's belt and handed it to him. Micah held it in his hands, sheepishly avoiding the Colonel's smiling face

"Now, Micah," the Colonel said, addressing him as Pride continued to enjoy his attention, "I would consider it a great favor if you would return to my kennel tomorrow mornin' to tend to Pride's needs just like you been doin'. He misses you, boy."

Micah looked directly into the Colonel's face.

"My name is Micah, sir."

The Colonel blinked and withdrew the cigar from his mouth, staring at Micah in disbelief.

"Why, of course, uh, M-Micah," he said hesitatingly.

"Somethin' else," Micah continued. "That's my friend, Isaac, they got down there in that jail in Tupelo. He'd be a lot better off if you could find some work at your place, instead of makin' him work on a chain gang."

The Colonel was taken aback. He had expected a more grateful response to his offer. Feeling slightly humiliated, he made a move to return to his car.

"I'll look into the matter," he said, then paused as Alexander opened the door. "Is that a 'yes' to my offer?"

Micah looked at his mother, who smiled back at him and nodded.

"I think we can work somethin' out ... ," Micah replied.

The Colonel looked at him with a frown.

" ... *sir*," Micah added.

Nodding, the Colonel pushed Pride aside and seated himself next to him as Alexander closed the door.

"Somethin' else I wonder, sir," Micah continued as the Colonel sat impatiently while Alexander cranked the car engine. "You still think the same way about colored folks like you was tellin' me the other day? 'Cause, I been givin' it a lot of thought. See, I been learnin' a lot from Pride there, and he taught me somethin' pretty important, I think."

The Colonel waited for the rest of Micah's statement.

"Which is?" he asked impatiently.

"Well, sir," Micah finally continued, "he taught me that I'm somethin' special. *Me*. An' if even a dog can see that, why then ... "

Hannah raised her eyebrows.

Now the Colonel was irritated again.

"Let's go, Alexander," he commanded.

"I'll be at the kennel bright an' early tomorrow mornin'," Micah called as the Colonel's car pulled away, then added again, "*sir.*"

As the car pulled away, Micah could see Pride looking back at him through the rear window. He remained in that position far into the distance.

"Micah," his mother said with a laugh, "I swear you got about as much nerve as a grizzly bear. You don't be careful, someday you're gonna get into big trouble!"

"He be alright," Jonah called through the screen door. "Get on in here. Let's open up the presents."

"Will you look at that!" Hannah exclaimed as they entered the house. Jonah had uncovered the ham, which sat conspicuously in the middle of the table. "Lord, how are we gonna eat all of that before it goes bad? Maybe we should take half of it down to the church."

"Momma," Micah said, "why couldn't we get half of it to Isaac when we see him?"

"Well you know," his mother said, "I think that's a good idea!"

Jonah and Hannah pulled up chairs around the Christmas tree as Micah and Annabel sat on the floor beside them, and each family member exchanged a gift with the other. Micah was presented with a new white shirt, which his mother had made for him, and she told him to save it to wear to church. He gave Annabel a book of paper dolls, and she gave him a copy of "The Call of the Wild."

"Course, I didn't have 'nuff money to pay for all of it," she confided, "Daddy and Momma helped some. It's about a dog."

Micah thanked her with a hug and then handed his gift to his father. Jonah playfully ripped off the wrapping.

"Oh," he said, after uncovering his gift. He seemed unsure of how to react. Finally, he said, "A fob for my watch. I shore been needin' that."

"I know," Micah said with a big smile. Jonah smiled back and began attaching it to his watch, careful not to reveal its condition.

Micah stood and approached his mother, reaching deep into his pocket.

"Momma," he said. "I feel real bad. I was savin' up to buy you that dress I saw you lookin' at over at the department store window a few weeks back, but then, when I saw Pride that first time at the depot, I couldn't think of nothin' but him, day and night. I even thought 'bout usin' the money I'd saved to buy me a dog just like him 'stead of buyin' you that dress. Now I'm ashamed, and I'm sorry I didn't get the dress bought, but I want you to have the money now. You can go down there and buy it if it's still there."

His eyes had become watery, and he withdrew a badly worn envelope containing paper and coin and handed it to his mother. She took it from him and held it to her breast, smiling at him with pride then she stood and retrieved a cigar box from a top shelf in the kitchen area. Returning to her chair, she opened the lid.

"I've been keepin' this old cigar box up there on the shelf for a long time now," she said to Micah softly. "Every time I find myself with a few extra pennies, I toss 'em in and close the lid. I haven't had much money to put in here for a while now, things bein' how they been."

Jonah looked down at the floor.

"Micah," she said, "I'm putin' this money you're givin' me into this box."

"But I want you to buy that dress!" Micah protested. "That's s'posed to be just for you!"

"Oh, it's for me alright," she said. "There's one thing I want more than any old dress or a thousand dresses, and that's what the money in this box is for. My dream is for you to go to college, and then Annabel too, soon as you're done. That's the greatest gift I could ever receive. And I'll bet you somethin'. You get your education because then … then I'll betcha you're gonna get yourself one of those collie dogs, just like Pride."

She grabbed Micah and embraced him.

"Dreams aren't always impossible," she told him. "Some of us just have to work harder to make 'em come true."

She squeezed him tightly.

"I'll keep right on dreamin'," she said, "if you will."

ALL THE GUNS FELL SILENT

The winter of 1914 along the Western Front had grown cold, wet, and stagnant amid the stretch of No Man's Land that separated the trenches of the Imperial German Army from the British Expeditionary Force. The soldiers who occupied the front lines of both armies had grown bored and lethargic. Fighting had reached a stalemate after the first desperate battles waged at the beginning of the conflict the summer before that had resulted in much blood spilled with little gain.

For the members of the Royal Sussex Brigade occupying the trenches near Ypres, the War to End All Wars consisted of small, compulsory night raids, sniper fire and sporadic artillery fire. The raids included repair of the barbed wire barrier strung between the opposing trenches. Sniper fire was dominated by the Germans, due to their position, which held the higher ground requiring the British to remain well protected behind eight-foot trenches and banked earth parapets. Artillery fire claimed the largest number of lives. Whizzing overhead or sometimes exploding short of their target, the shells flew so often that none of the men paid much attention except on that rare occasion when one would land close enough to take a life or cause a serious injury.

Corporal Fraser was a victim of such an injury, and his chances of survival were slim. Sergeant Pike, displaying no emotion, looked inside the small bunker, where the young recruit lay moaning in pain while a young private tried to persuade him to drink water from a canteen.

" 'e can't take much more o' this pain, Sarge," the young recruit said.

Casting him a cursory glance, the sergeant left. Making his way toward his commanding officer's bunker, he made no eye contact with his men who all sat along the edges of the trench, cold, damp and depressed, engulfed in mud and foul smells in the late-night darkness. A few were playing cards, and some cleaned rifles, while others leaned against sandbags, attempting to sleep. Many smoked cigarettes. All hung their heads low as light rain, dismal and persistent, dripped from the brim of their helmets.

Kicking a lingering rat out of the way, Pike brushed aside the canvas curtain that hung over the doorway of Second Lieutenant Harris's bunker and found the thirty-six-year-old officer seated at a wooden slab supported by sandbags. He was making entries in a pocket-size notebook as he drank from a metal cup, occasionally refreshing it with liquid from a small flask, which, Pike noted was not military issue.

"Sir," Pike addressed him.

"What is the condition of our casualty, sergeant?" Harris asked.

"I doubt he'll be able to hold on much longer, sir," Pike replied. "He's lost a lot of blood, and he probably hasn't the strength to withstand the pain."

"Hmm," mused the lieutenant. He gestured to the field telephone that sat on a sandbag nearby. "Well, I had contact with the Regimental Medical Officer before the telephone line went dead, and I'm afraid the news is not encouraging. As we've observed, the Jerries' accuracy is improving. They've blown several sizeable holes in our communication trench, which quickly filled with rainwater and sludge, making it nearly impossible for anyone to get a stretcher through and back. They tell me they're working on it. In the meantime, we need to keep Corporal Fraser warm to try to prevent shock."

"I'm afraid shock has already set in, sir."

"I'm not surprised. There is one small glimmer of hope I can report. They're sending us a Red Cross dog with some morphine. Hopefully, that will provide Fraser with some relief until we can get him transported out."

"Gracie perhaps?" Pike asked. He recalled that the little tri-colored rough collie had been sent up to their location through the communication trench on several past occasions to make medical deliveries. Her very presence provided the men with an antidote to their gloom no mere medicine could bestow, and they had all become quite fond of her.

Harris paused, furrowing his brow and sipping from his cup. "I do worry, though," he continued. "The dog will have to travel several miles to get here, and she won't be traveling through the trenches. To save time, they're sending her through on a more direct route. She'll be trying to reach us directly through No Man's Land."

"That's quite a risk," Pike declared.

"Yes. Well, perhaps that's why they're sending a dog. More expendable than a soldier, I suppose."

Pike nodded in agreement. Neither man spoke for several seconds.

"Sit down, sergeant," the lieutenant said, nodding toward an overturned bucket nearby.

"Thank you, sir," Pike replied as he seated himself opposite his superior officer, who produced a second tin cup and prepared to pour from his flask.

"Join me in a bit of holiday celebration, won't you?" Harris offered.

"None for me, Sir," Pike hastily replied, holding up his hand. He nodded toward a nearby coffee pot. "A bit of that coffee will suffice if it's still warm."

"Come now, sergeant," the lieutenant coaxed. "have you forgotten it's Christmas Eve? Relax a bit, why don't you?"

"Thank you, no, sir," Pike said as he leaned across the table to pour from the coffee pot. "War doesn't pause for holidays."

The lieutenant studied the sergeant's face for a moment before asking, "How old are you, Sergeant Pike? Forty-two perhaps?"

Pike nodded. "Close enough."

"I've only been with this unit a few weeks. You were in the fighting quite heavy last month, weren't you?"

"Indeed, sir," Pike responded, with no other visible reaction.

"I must commend you on your ability to remain calm and unfettered regardless of the situation."

Pike held out his hand, palm facing downward. It was rock-solid steady. "Always, sir."

"I've faced combat myself, but I don't think I've ever met a more even-tempered soldier than you. How on earth do you manage it?"

"Quite simple, sir. I learned long ago never to allow myself compassion or sentiment. There's no room for it. Tomorrow I may have to blow off the heads of an entire battalion of Jerries. Tonight I may have to sacrifice one of my own men over the top. Maybe all of them, if I'm given the order. I can't perform my job efficiently if I spend any time thinking about it. Neither can I mourn over lives lost. Things like that will only cloud my judgment if I dwell on them."

"But surely," Harris said with amazement, "you can't abandon all humanity …"

"Excuse me, sir," Pike interrupted. "War by its very nature is inhumane, isn't it?"

Harris was flustered. "But Christmas Eve … Even in war there has to be time out for humanity."

"That's not been my experience," Pike said, taking a sip of coffee. "and I endure it for the sake of the home front. Let England enjoy the luxury of sentimentality. There's no place for it on the front line."

The lieutenant was about to debate the topic further when they were abruptly interrupted by a corporal. His entrance was punctuated by the sound of gunfire from both sides of the trenches.

"Sir," the soldier reported. "There's movement."

"Aaah," Harris said, taking one last swig from his cup and putting on his cap as both men stood. "That'll be Gracie."

The rain had stopped as the two men rushed to the central location of their post, paying little notice of the soldiers who rose and stood at attention as they passed. They quickly reached their destination, where a loophole had been cut into the parapet, enabling them to better assess the activity taking place beyond the trenches. The hole was normally covered with a metal plate to prevent sniper fire from penetrating the barrier but as they arrived, a soldier was utilizing a makeshift wooden trench periscope to view the activity outside without facing exposure. The gunfire had stopped.

"Let me take a look, Steadwell," the lieutenant ordered as he stepped forward and was handed the periscope. He slowly surveyed the landscape.

"Send up a flare," he called out, and one of the soldiers complied.

"I heard her yip, Sarge," Steadwell said, "when she got hit."

"She's been hit?" Sargent Pike asked. The soldier nodded.

"There she is," Harris said. "It's Gracie alright. She's trying to stand, but she can't."

"She can't," he repeated as he turned his face away from the periscope.

"We'll need to send someone out to get the morphine," Pike said. Quickly turning, he called out the names of three of the closest men standing nearby.

"Hold on," Harris ordered, having resumed observation through the telescope.

There was silence for the next minute.

"What in God's name is going on out there?" the lieutenant wondered.

A voice was heard from the German trenches.

"My name is Oberleutnat Ludendorff," the voice called out with only a slight German dialect. "I would like to speak with your commanding officer. Can we talk?"

"I'll talk to him," Pike said with anger in his voice as he stepped forward and withdrew his sidearm.

"Stay where you are, sergeant," the lieutenant commanded.

"This is Second Lieutenant Harris speaking," he yelled back to the German. "What do you want to speak about?" "Your Red Cross canine," the voice replied. "He is badly wounded. I have a man here with veterinary experience. Perhaps he can help."

Sergeant Pike frowned.

"Why in God's name would you wish to help your enemy?" Harris shouted.

There was a moment of silence before Ludendorff replied, in a softer voice, "It is Christmas Eve."

Harris considered the offer before responding.

"While you're considering his compassionate offer, sir," Pike said, leaning in close. "Remember, this is the German Army you're dealing with here. This is the army that massacred well over a thousand unarmed, innocent men, women and children in the Belgium villages just a few short months ago. Reservists of the most distinguished regiments of the Prussian army murdered them all without mercy and for absolutely no reason. Why would they declare a Christmas truce to save their enemy's dog? Not likely, sir."

Ludendorff called out again. "I'm going to trust your honor, Lieutenant. I'm stepping out of our trench. I am unarmed. I will have one man with me. We will approach *der hund* to see if any assistance can be given. My men have been ordered to hold their fire, and they will not shoot unless you shoot first. Agreed?"

Harris did not immediately reply but trained the periscope on the opposite trench, which lay a distance of approximately 150 yards across a muddy, cratered field, strung with strands of barbed wire.

"Fire another flare," he ordered.

As the field was illuminated, Harris could clearly see a German officer climbing from the trench in the distance. When he reached the summit, he slowly stepped forward, his hands held out from his side to indicate he was not holding a weapon. He was closely followed by another soldier, who was carrying a small leather bag.

"Sir!" Pike cautioned.

Harris studied him a moment before speaking. "Find out if there is anyone in our unit with any kind of veterinary experience. Any kind of background working with animals."

"Excuse me, sir," Steadwell interjected. "Private Hawthorne. He's studying to be a zoologist. Comes from a long line of farmers, he says. Midwife to cows, sheep, pigs. You get the idea, sir."

"Private Hawthorne!" the sergeant interrupted. "Report!"

The word went out down the line, and a few moments later a lanky, red-faced, bespectacled, twenty-three-year-old private appeared, a rifle slung over his shoulder.

"Private Hawthorne reporting, Sergeant Pike!" he said.

"Come with us. Keep your weapon on your shoulder unless provoked," Harris ordered before issuing a command to his men. "Now listen to me! All of you. You are to hold your fire unless, and *only* unless the Germans fire first. Understood?"

"Understood, sir!" a corporal replied.

"Alright. Let's go," he said to Pike and Hawthorne nervously as he ascended a ladder propped next to the loophole.

After breaching the parapet, Lieutenant Harris paused to allow his men to join him. Pike stepped forward with a pair of wire cutters and opened a gap in the barbed wire through which they cautiously passed.

Reaching the center of the field, they found the German officer standing with his fingers in his belt. He appeared to be in his mid-thirties and greeted them with a friendly smile. An older soldier was kneeling next to the collie, who was panting at a very rapid pace. Her eyes were open wide and blood soaked the Red Cross vest she wore. The soldier said a few words in German to his commander who passed on his message to his men in the trench.

"We are fetching the dog some water," he explained to Harris.

Sergeant Pike eyed everyone suspiciously and never removed his grasp from the handle of the sidearm in his holster.

Private Hawthorne stepped forward, unslinging his rifle and laying it down beside him as he knelt next to the dog. He inspected her closely, before looking up at the veterinarian, who slowly shook his head.

"I wish I could be optimistic, sir," he said to the lieutenant, "but I don't see that there's anything that can be done."

Suddenly Sergeant Pike stepped forward and brusquely unfastened the pocket on the side of the dog's vest, withdrawing a small bottle.

"This will be the medicine," he said. "I'll take that."

Noticing that Ludendorff was eyeing him suspiciously, Pike held the vial high for the lieutenant's inspection.

"Medicine. Morphine" he said, and then called out over his shoulder. "Private Steadwell!"

The young soldier clambered over the parapet and rushed to them.

"Get this to Fraser, but be careful." Pike said, handing him the bottle. "Don't give it all to him at one time. It must be rationed. Now move. On the double!"

Two German soldiers came forward, one of them carefully bearing a tin bowl of water. They handed it to the veterinarian who set it down in front of the collie.

When she made no move to drink, Hawthorne gently lifted her head, but the movement caused a soft whine of pain so he laid her head back down. She softly licked his hand in gratitude.

Withdrawing his other hand from beneath her neck, he could feel a metal canister, about eight centimeters long, lying beneath her body, unseen by the others. He had observed her bearing the canister on her previous missions to the British trenches. He knew it would contain a message. Observed by the German soldiers, Hawthorne made the choice to say nothing for the moment.

The veterinarian pulled a rag from his pocket, dampened it in the water dish and wiped at the mud and blood on the dog's face and neck. He asked Ludendorff a question.

"*Morphium*," the officer replied.

The veterinarian sighed and spoke again.

"The morphine," Ludendorff translated. "He says it could be used to help the dog's pain."

"It must be used for our wounded soldier," Harris told him. "Would it help save the dog's life?"

"No," the German replied. "Will it save your soldier's life?"

"No," Harris admitted. "The only way the soldier will live is if he gets treatment soon, but the morphine will help him survive the pain until, if or when help arrives."

The men gathered around the fallen dog, watching her with hopelessness.

"If that's the case, we'd best put Gracie out of her misery," Pike said, starting to lift his pistol from its holster.

The veterinarian, who had been kneeling next to the dog, immediately fell back on his haunches, and the other soldiers all grabbed their weapons in response.

"No! Wait!" Harris said, stepping in and holding up his hand to them. "Not for you! For the dog."

He pointed to Gracie to indicate his sergeant's intention. It made no difference. The men held their weapons a little higher.

"*Nein!*" the veterinarian yelled, holding up his hand.

Ludendorff and Harris both instructed their men to stand down, and all reluctantly obliged.

"It's the humane thing to do, sir," Pike said.

"The *humane* thing, you say?" Harris asked sarcastically. "Is there room for such sentiment on the battlefield, Sergeant Pike?"

He hesitated to reply.

Harris knew Pike was right, but he was hesitant to take action if the veterinarian thought it wasn't quite time.

"Return to the trench," he ordered Pike. "See how Fraser is progressing. Make sure he's been given the proper dose."

"Sir!" the sergeant replied and turned to go.

"*Warten!*" one of the two German soldiers called to him. The soldier held up an empty cigarette case and spoke to him in German, pointing to the British line.

"They want to know if any of your men can spare a cigarette," Ludendorff said with a smile.

Harris smiled back. "Send a couple of the men back with cigarettes," he told Pike.

The sergeant stared back to him in disbelief.

"Christmas," Ludendorff said to him apologetically.

Pike turned away angrily and headed back to the trench.

"Where did you learn your English?" Harris asked his German counterpart as they stood over the fallen dog. "It's quite good."

"I was born in Frankfurt, but I spent a great deal of my youth in Brighton. My father was drawn into German politics, and my family returned home several years ago. Ahh, what I wouldn't give for a pint at the Druid's Head tonight."

"Brighton? Druid's Head?" Harris asked, laughing. "I frequented the place often. Why haven't we met before? Here." Pulling his flask from his coat pocket, he offered it to Ludendorff. "Christmas," he reminded him.

From that point the two men conversed like old friends, sharing memories and mutual acquaintances. As they conversed, Private Steadwell returned with three other soldiers. The men offered cigarettes to the Germans as Steadwell knelt next to Hawthorne, speaking to him quietly as he looked over his shoulder toward Lieutenant Harris, to make certain he was not observed.

It started slowly at first, but then steadily began to build. Observing their two commanders laughing and sharing a drink, it wasn't long before other soldiers from both sides gradually began meeting on the terrain they called No Man's Land.

Before mingling, the men from both armies first paid homage to Gracie, stroking her fur softly and offering loving, encouraging words. One British soldier, overcome with emotion, leaned over her, his face on hers, crying unabashedly. A German soldier approached and placed his hand tenderly on his shoulder. Looking up at the man who, but a short while ago had been his enemy, he allowed the soldier to help him to his feet where they shared a German beverage.

When Sergeant Pike climbed out of the trench a while later, he was infuriated to see large numbers of men from both armies intermingling, exchanging what small gifts they had to offer including liquor, cigarettes and food, swapping stories and sharing photos of loved ones. A cheer went up as the hour passed midnight, and the men erupted in a chorus of "Auld Lang Syne" followed by Christmas carols, everyone singing together but in their own tongues.

Pike found Harris with Oberleutnat Ludendorff, seated on wooden chairs supplied from the German bunker. They were smoking, sharing stories and a bottle of whiskey.

"Sir, if I may," Pike began, barely concealing his rage.

"You will, whether I say yay or nay, I'm sure," Harris replied with a chuckle.

"Sir, have you considered how Major Richardson will react when he finds out we've been fraternizing with the enemy?"

"In fact, Sergeant Pike," Harris responded, very much under the influence, "It's been reported that many other battalions all up and down the front have declared a sort of temporary truce, and that's, let me see, how many miles between the North Sea to the mountain frontiers of Switzerland? Anyway, that would be quite a lot of soldiers to court-martial, don't you think?"

He looked at Gracie, who still lay not far away. A makeshift shelter of canvas suspended between four poles had been erected overhead and a small campfire was burning nearby to keep her warm. Several men sat in a circle around her, keeping vigil as they sang or hummed songs, occasionally reaching out to touch her.

"Strange to think, isn't it?" Harris said, in a voice that sounded quite sober as he stared at her. "It all seems to have started right here with Gracie and then spread down the line. Look at her now. She's lying so quiet and still. I don't think she's in as much pain as she was. You were wrong to want to put her out of her misery, sergeant. I think she's found comfort with us here. I think it's relieved her pain."

Pike clenched his jaw and turned to leave but stopped and turned back after taking only a couple of steps.

"Sir, I need to talk to you for a moment." He looked at Ludendorff. "Alone, if I may."

The lieutenant shrugged and joined his sergeant out of ear-shot of the German.

"I've dispatched two men behind our line to convey Corporal Fraser to the field hospital," Pike revealed in a quiet voice. "The communication trench may not be usable, but with this, uh, temporary truce, they should be able to transport him by stretcher above ground without the Germans taking notice."

Harris was impressed. "Good thinking, Sergeant Pike." Placing an arm around the sergeant's shoulder he advised, "Now, will you kindly remove that stick lodged up your ass and join your men in celebrating Christmas, if only for just a little while? Here, go pet Gracie for a few moments. It will do you good."

Pike looked away from the dog. "I can't do that, sir. With respect."

The lieutenant couldn't help but notice that Pike seemed to be trying to suppress emotion as he rushed back to the trench.

The night passed quickly. Several weeks of mild but miserably soaking weather had given way overnight to sudden hard frost giving the area a dusting of ice and snow that glowed as daybreak also revealed a sky clear and bright.

The soldiers joined around campfires scattered about No

Man's Land, as they shared what breakfast they could manage to improvise.

Suddenly a British soldier rushed into the middle of the gatherings and yelled, "Look what I found!" as he tossed a football high into the air. A hearty cheer went up among the men as they rushed to improvise teams and lay out a game field, moving barbed wire aside to provide room.

From the spot where he lay beside Gracie, Private Hawthorne looked up at the commotion nearby. Many men had dropped by to visit the dog throughout the night, but he had never left her side, watching her breathing and doing his best to comfort her. He remained alert for an opening to secure the message canister that still lay hidden beneath her, but there was always a German soldier present, so he continued to wait.

Sergeant Pike suddenly appeared beside him and tapped him on the shoulder. "Did you do as I ordered?" he asked.

"I wasn't seen," Hawthorne replied with a nod.

"Come on, Private. Take a break. Go watch the game. It doesn't look like it can be stopped, God help us all," Pike said bitterly.

"Thank you, Sarge," Hawthorne replied. "I couldn't leave her, not after all she's done for us."

After some hesitation, Pike slowly squatted next to him.

"Go ahead. Touch her," Hawthorne encouraged. "After all she's done for us, don't you think that's the least you can do for her?"

The sergeant looked at him angrily and started to rise, but gradually relaxed and forced himself to look at the dog. Unable to control himself, he slowly reached out and began stroking her fur.

"Amazing, isn't it?" Hawthorne remarked. "Most dogs

prefer the company of man over their own species. A long time ago our ancestors sought out the other animals of the wild and tamed them to serve, but the dog came to us of his own accord, almost as if to say, 'I am here to do your bidding. You will be my god, and I will hunt with you, I will risk my life to protect you and the ones you love, and I will quietly comfort you. I will do all of this and more and demand nothing in return.'

"When Gracie was sent to deliver the medicine, she sensed the danger, but she obeyed unconditionally because it was her nature. Even now, she holds no grudge, does she? Not even against the Germans."

"You should have enlisted as a chaplain," Pike said sarcastically.

"I could never provide the spiritual comfort Gracie has given us this Christmas. She brought us all together, didn't she, Sarge?"

Pike slowly became aware that his eyes were filling with tears. He stopped stroking the dog's fur. Regaining his tough outer shell, he swiftly pulled his hand back.

"I can't do this," he said and abruptly walked away.

As the day wore on, the unreality of their experience began to slowly consume the consciousness of the men. Abandonment eventually gave way to restraint and good cheer to melancholy. The day would soon be over, they silently reminded themselves, and tomorrow would bring the return of death and dying, and the memory of the festivities they had enjoyed would have to be forgotten if they were to survive the madness that lay ahead. While they sat resting around the campfires, exhausted from their merrymaking, silently watching the sun set in the early evening, they were suddenly snapped back to reality as death returned.

"She's gone," Hawthorne said, his voice breaking the stillness.

At first, the men failed to comprehend what he was saying, but as the import of his words settled in, all of them rose to their feet and surrounded the little shelter where Gracie lay. They stood there in silence, each of them enduring the heartache of the moment as best they could. Although they had all experienced the loss of dear comrades on the battlefield and in the trenches, and though they knew they would endure many more, the sorrow of that moment was somehow different.

"She never harmed anyone," a voice from within the group was heard to say. "She wasn't fighting. She was only obeying the command she was given. She was just trying to save a life. She didn't deserve to die."

The men were joined by their two commanding officers, who both wore a mutual expression of exhaustion.

Hawthorne and the German veterinarian were seated on the ground on opposite sides of the dog. The Englishman held his breath as the German attempted a farewell gesture by stroking the fur around Gracie's neck. He stopped as his fingers discovered the leather strap that had been concealed by her thick fur and then started to remove it. Soon he began tugging at the strap, realizing that it was connected to something beneath her. With little effort, he lifted the canister before him.

Acting fast, Hawthorne grabbed the object, catching the German unaware.

"Sir!" he called out, speedily tossing it to Lieutenant Harris.

Surprised, Harris caught the item with both hands and

held it against his chest as he dropped his flask.

"What is that?" Oberleutnat Ludendorff asked, pointing.

Harris didn't answer.

"I know what it is," Ludendorff realized. "It is a message from your commanding officer. Special orders perhaps, advising you of troop movements, or reinforcements."

"I doubt that it ... ," Harris began.

Ludendorff held out his hand. "Would you be kind enough to share it with me, Lieutenant? In the spirit of Christmas?"

Harris stood hesitating. "That isn't fair."

"Don't be absurd," Ludendorff scoffed.

After hesitating a moment, Harris began unscrewing the lid on the container. Reaching inside, he withdrew a folded piece of paper and held it before him.

"Oberleutnat Ludendorff," he said, "I am now going to return to my bunker where I will read this message privately."

"In that case," Ludendorff snapped back, "I must order you to remain where you are."

Quickly removing his sidearm from its holster, he aimed it at Harris as the men of both armies immediately rushed to join their leaders, falling into place in groups opposing each other. Those who still had their rifles unslung them and pointed them at their opposite number as the others all scrambled to reclaim their weapons. Ammunition was chambered, creating a chorus of metallic clicks. A standoff had begun.

Ludendorff cast a glance toward his men.

"Let me see," he said. "Shall I begin a countdown? On the count of three either you hand over that paper or my men will open fire on your men."

"And my men will do the same," Harris replied evenly. "Nearly everyone on this field will die. Are you prepared for that?"

"Are you?" Ludendorff countered, aiming his pistol at Harris' head.

"One!" he called.

Harris stood his ground. No one moved.

Suddenly, several of the British soldiers were pushed aside as Sergeant Pike interrupted the countdown and stood between the two officers. His sidearm was in its holster.

"This is madness!" he yelled at the two men. "Look at the two of you. One minute you're brothers celebrating the birth of your Lord and Savior and the next preparing to annihilate each other and all your men!"

"I'm afraid that's the nature of war," Ludendorff responded, half amused at the sergeant's reaction.

"It will be once again the nature of war at dusk," Pike replied. "But for now ..."

Suddenly turning to face Harris he unexpectedly snatched the note from his hand. Continuing to face the lieutenant, he unfolded the paper and read its contents silently. The energy in his body deflated. He held the note up for Harris to read. He reacted similarly.

"May I share this information with the enemy?" Pike asked. Harris looked away, nodding.

Pike turned and faced the German officer and read aloud, "The message is from headquarters and it reads, 'Mercy, peace, and love be yours in abundance. Jude, first chapter, second verse.'"

Ludendorff looked at him in disbelief. Pike handed him the paper.

After reading the note, he slowly holstered his weapon and handed the note back as one of his men yelled a command for German soldiers to lower their weapons.

"Stand down, men," Pike ordered his men before addressing Ludendorff again.

"And for this," Pike said holding up the message for both officers to see, "for this you and all of your men were prepared to kill and be killed."

Neither man could look at the other.

While both officers stood in shame, Pike whispered in Harris' ear. "I have news for you, sir."

The two men distanced themselves to a place they would not be overheard.

"The two men have returned from the field hospital," Pike told him. "The doctor thinks there's a good chance Corporal Fraser will pull through."

"Thank God," Harris said.

"Also, there is a message from Major Richardson," Pike continued. "We are to cease fraternization with the enemy immediately and return to our posts. Anyone who fails to follow his order will be court-martialed."

"Thank you, sergeant," Harris replied with a nod. "For everything."

"One more thing," Pike added. "We are to prepare ourselves for an all-out assault on the German entrenchments. Soon."

"Right," Harris acknowledged as he looked toward Gracie. "But there is something we must do first."

A cold rain began to fall as the British and German soldiers laid Gracie to rest, and Second Lieutenant Harris read a few passages from the Bible, ending with the Lord's Prayer.

A rustic wooden cross had been fixed to her grave to which Sergeant Pike nailed the note that Gracie had delivered.

Without looking at each other, the men drifted back to their positions in the trenches.

As Private Hawthorne passed, Harris, standing next to Pike at Gracie's grave, called out to him.

"You did an admirable job tending to our Gracie," Harris told him. "She appeared to be resting peacefully throughout the ordeal."

"Yes, sir," Hawthorne said, uncomfortable with the discussion.

"I wonder, though," Harris continued, "if she would have been quite as comfortable if you hadn't administered that dose of morphine, that small amount someone was able to withhold from Corporal Fraser."

Hawthorne squirmed. "Will that be all, sir?"

"May I trust that you received authorization to appropriate that dosage from an individual of higher rank?"

"That will be all, Private Hawthorne. Report to your station immediately," Pike interjected.

"Yes, Sergeant Pike," Hawthorne said, beating a hasty retreat.

Harris smiled at Pike, and the two men began casually strolling back to their trenches.

"Amazing, the things we learn from animals like Gracie simply by being in their presence, isn't it, Sergeant Pike? Things like humanity, for example."

The war raged on for several years more, claiming an unimaginable number of deaths. The wooden cross on Gracie's grave stood tall throughout, and continually waving in the breeze of combat was the piece of paper on which was written the message she had delivered that Christmas 1914.

A DREAM FOR CHRISTMAS

There is a story I tell my children and grandchildren every Christmas Eve. Like the original story of the first Christmas, I cannot vouch for its veracity, but like the original story, its retelling is more important than its authenticity. Tonight, with children gathered about me in the comfort of my front room and with the embers in the fireplace glowing softly, the tale begins to unfold once more.

Resting together under our Christmas tree, there are three rough collies.

There is the twelve-year-old old collie with the honey sable coat and the long silver and white muzzle. Lying next to him is the six-year-old female collie with the single blue eye and the brown, sable marbling with the single white star atop her head, and nearby lies the five-year-old mahogany-colored young collie with the dazzling white ruff.

All of them lie deeply enveloped in sleep, and in that sleep, they all share the same, familiar, singular dream.

No one knows exactly on which date the collie first appeared among the sheep in the fields of Scotland, nor can we be certain where they originated, but the genesis of the breed is of no interest to the collies who sleep before my tree. In their communal dream they are transported centuries into the past to a hillside overlooking the little ancient town of Bethlehem, and it is there that their favorite dream begins.

As the shades of evening drew on, the flock for which the

collies were responsible had settled in for the night, with the silence broken only by the occasional bleat or the soft clanging of a sheep's bell as it shifted itself for comfort.

The stars that blanketed the sky all gleamed noticeably brighter that night more than ever before, and the eyes of the collies searched the heavens for some meaning to a mysterious sensation that consumed them with increasing strength as the night engulfed all.

"Do you feel it, too?" the young collie asked.

"Yes," replied the female. "So strange!"

"This is a special night, and it will lead to an even more special day tomorrow," the old collie declared. "Come. We must have permission to investigate this."

The other two collies knew better than to ask him how he knew. They respected his wisdom and did not question.

A young shepherd sat nearby on a rock, carving an object from a piece of wood he held in his hand as he too, marveled at the brilliance of the sky. The light that shone from the heavens was bright enough that he needed no additional illumination to judge how well his carving was progressing. He held the figure of a small lamb close to his face to inspect the results of his work.

As he continued to finish off his model, the collies approached him. The young collie placed a paw on the shepherd's knee, and all three dogs looked at him with an expression that he recognized. They were asking his permission to leave the flock for a while. They would be back, he knew, but they had never before made such a request this late at night. Nevertheless, he knew the reason for their request.

Something was happening in the quiet little village at the

bottom of the hill. The shepherd sensed it as strongly as they did, and he knew they wanted to satisfy their curiosity. He nodded his head in approval, and the three collies joyfully raced down the hill.

As they neared the town, they slowed their pace, attempting to determine where the source of the mystery lay. They found no activity in the town that night. All was unusually quiet, but peering around the corner of a mud hut into a narrow cobblestone street, they observed, not very far away, a young man conversing with another man at the doorway of an inn.

The proprietor was adamantly shaking his head, signifying that he had no rooms available. The man continued to plead with the landlord, gesturing toward the woman with him, who sat upon a small, tired donkey. There was no mistaking that the woman was with child, but the innkeeper could not be persuaded to admit the couple. Soon he closed his door.

The man, drained of energy and hope, leaned against the door and buried his face in the hollow of his elbow. The lady on the donkey reached her arm out to him, and he turned to face her. Seeing the outstretched hand and her kind, smiling face, he found the strength to join her and kissed her palm.

The two younger dogs turned to the old collie for guidance

"I know where they can find shelter," he said. "Come!"

They followed as he led them to the young couple. The man was looking back at the street they had just traveled, struggling with indecision, and he didn't notice the three dogs that approached him from the front. It wasn't until he felt the young collie's muzzle touch the hand that held the donkey's reins that he became aware of their presence.

As the man watched with amazement, the young collie took the reins in his mouth and softly started to pull them from his hand. He was not inclined to release his hold until the lady touched his shoulder. He looked up and saw she was smiling her approval.

The reins were gradually released to the collie's control as he gently took the donkey down the street, following the old collie, as he led the way. The female walked beside the lady on one side while the husband, holding his wife's hand, traveled opposite.

Turning onto a smaller street, which was lined with many crowded two-story dwellings, the old collie eventually led them down a narrow alley that delivered them into an open area, where there stood a modest, wooden stable.

An old man was seated in front on a small stool, wearily milking a cow that was eating hay spread out before her as a small calf nibbled at a patch of grass nearby. The young collie brought the donkey to a halt as the old collie approached the old man.

The cow stopped eating and turned her head, greeting the visitors with a soft low, which captured the attention of the old man. Squinting in the lamplight, he managed to recognize the old collie, and his eyes became slits as his wrinkled face burst into a joyous smile.

The old collie approached the man, who greeted him as an old friend, heaping words of bountiful love and affection. Gradually he became aware of the others in his presence, and he humbly welcomed them. He explained that as he was settling into sleep, a dream had revealed to him that a very special event would be taking place in his stable in the early morning, so he felt it would be best to milk his cow now in case the activities he had dreamed about prevented him from doing so the next day.

Noticing the lady's condition, he chided the man for making her travel late at night, but he was soon informed of their inability to find lodgings and that the birth of their child was imminent.

The old man was outraged that no one had managed to find accommodations for them in such a situation and apologized that his own wretched dwelling was dirty and foul, pronouncing it as unfit for the birth of a child. He declared that his stable was more pleasant than his own home.

With an eye to his wife's discomfort and the hardship she had already endured, the husband pleaded with him to allow them to make use of his stable, just for the night. The old man protested, but when the old collie nudged his hand and looked at him with pleading eyes, he consented.

The old man helped prepare the stable, laying down straw for the lady to lie upon, and the collies herded the cow, horses, donkey and sheep to make room for the lodgers. The husband assisted his wife.

After they had settled in, the old man apologized that he could not do more for them and excused himself. After he had gone, all of the animals remained, watching over the young couple.

"There is one thing missing," the female collie declared and then turned to the cow. "Will you be kind enough to help me, please?" she asked.

The other collies joined them as the female led them to a corner of the stable. Pulling aside tools, harnesses, wooden boxes and debris that were lying in a heap, she uncovered the item she was seeking and busied herself supervising the cow, furnishing the item with the softest straw that could be found. When she was certain all had been prepared to her liking, she called for the other collies to help her, and together, using their teeth, they dragged the object to the center of the stable.

All of the animals vocalized their approval of the makeshift cradle that had been created out of a small wooden manger filled with straw.

The collies were pleased to see that the look of worry on the man's face had been replaced with a smile and a look of relief. The lady beamed and whispered a silent "thank you" to all of the animals.

"We must bring the shepherd here," the old collie decided. Together the dogs departed.

They found the shepherd sitting on the ground leaning against a large rock near his sheep, still holding the little carving in his hand. He was still awake, and a look of awe and wonder was upon his face as he sat gazing toward the heavens. Before him he beheld a miraculous star, shining beautiful and bright over the town of Bethlehem, and it seemed to beckon him to the stable.

The young collie tugged at his sleeve. The sheep lay peacefully on the hillside, and the shepherd was filled with a spirit of calmness that told him he need have no worry leaving them for a while. It made him feel that something was there, unseen, watching over his flock and that they would remain undisturbed until he returned. He followed the collies down the hillside as if in a dream, led by the light in the heavens.

Arriving back at the stable, they found several other shepherds all gathered around the wide entryway, looking upon its occupants with reverence.

The shepherd and his collies found a place among the

onlookers. Their eyes widened as they beheld the young woman cradling a newborn infant in her arms, her husband by her side. The loving mother's face glowed with a vision of tenderness and humble pride. The collies had never seen a human infant before, and they were transfixed by the sight.

While they watched, the lady moved forward and delicately laid her child in the manger and then seated herself beside it. Looking up at the gathering by the entry, her eyes fell on the collies. She beckoned to them.

Quietly moving forward, they peered over the top of the manger, fascinated by the infant. They remained transfixed for several minutes.

"If only we had a gift to give to the child," the female said.

The young collie considered her comment for a moment before turning from the makeshift cradle. Approaching his shepherd, the young collie nudged the hand that still held the woodcarving of the lamb. Recognizing what the collie was asking, he allowed the dog to gently grasp the carving in his teeth.

The young collie returned to the manger and leaned over, laying the wooden lamb on the straw next to the child. The new mother smiled sweetly and softly stroked the collie's head.

As the early hours of the morning wore on, the visitors gradually departed. Only the collies lingered behind until dawn. They laid themselves in front of the manger, drifting in and out of sleep, protecting the child as they protected their flock.

They rested there, looking very much as they do now, on the floor of our front room. Looking closely, it's easy to imagine a manger in place of the tree and the gifts of the magi can be envisioned in place of our family presents. And before all of it, the Christmas Collies lay sharing their Christmas dream.

That's the story we tell every Yuletide, and now it's time for all to turn in to sleep and dream of the day to come. But first, I must share something very special that has been in our family for many, many generations. It stands on the mantle, ancient as the Christmas story itself, but perhaps barely recognizable these days from the centuries of wear and handling.

If one examines it carefully it is recognizable as a carving of a little lamb.

AFTERWORD

Although I had conceived the outline of "The Christmas Dress" nearly a year before I committed it to paper, I was very pleasantly surprised to discover, while putting the final touches to the manuscript, the true story of Dr. James McCain, an African American, who proved, against the odds, that Micah's dreams could come true.

Gayle Kaye is co-chair of the Collie Club of America Historian Committee and author of the books "The Collie in America" and "A Century of Collies." In telling the story of this amazing individual, Gayle has written, in part:

"Dr. James Price McCain, along with his wife Gertrude, owned the Cainbrooke Collies in Pittsburgh, Pennsylvania. Dr. McCain's story is especially remarkable because he was an African American taking part in a sport dominated by white men and women. He was a medical doctor, in an era when few black people were going to college, let alone going on to become doctors. On top of that, he was a highly successful Collie breeder and exhibitor and one of the most popular judges of his time. By his own admission, he was always a dog fancier. However, thanks to the Albert Payson Terhune books, his love affair with Collies began in 1927 with the purchase of a pet tri male of Bellhaven breeding. Dr. McCain's influence was profound and his overall contributions to the Collie breed were extraordinary!

"Born in Rockingham, North Carolina in 1892, Dr.

McCain or 'Doc' as his friends called him, was the son of a Methodist Minister, a former slave. His college education came at Livingstone College in North Carolina, getting his degree in 1913. He entered medical school at Howard University in Washington D.C. and graduated an MD in 1918. He interned at Freeman's Hospital in Washington D.C. and began general medical practice in 1920.

"Instrumental in National breed club affairs, Dr. McCain served the Collie Club of America in many capacities and at the time of his death, he was a first Vice President. He also authored and created a pamphlet for the club titled 'The Advantages of Collie Ownership.' Like everything else he did, it was extremely well done and his passion for Collies was unmistakable.

"Dr. McCain was the first African American to be licensed to judge by the American Kennel Club. This was quite an achievement for a man born the son of a slave! Today it is easy to forget that during the time he was breeding and showing, blacks did not have the same rights as white people and yet he managed to not only survive, but he flourished. By the late 1940s, he became an all-breed judge. Always popular and always in high demand, he judged from coast to coast. In 1949 his greatest dream came true when he was selected to judge the Collie Club of America Specialty in California. With an entry of 247, it was the largest National held up to that point, in the days when there was only one judge. At the show, he started Ch. Hazeljane's Bright Future onto a record-setting (4) consecutive Best of Breed wins. That night at the show banquet, when he was introduced for a short speech, he received a standing ovation. His final judging assignment, Best in Show at the Buffalo Kennel Club show, came two weeks before his death in 1957!

"This amazing gentleman wrote the following in a 1949 'Collie Review' article on his 'Once in a Lifetime' experience of judging the National Specialty:

" 'The words "Iron Curtain" may mean many things to many people. To a statesman, it might refer to the unknown political goings-on in that vast area known as the Russian sphere of influence. To average Mr. and Mrs. John Q. Citizen, it can mean the mystery of what goes on in the dressing room before the main fight ... or what the catcher is actually saying to the pitcher in the midst of a 9th inning rally ... or what is REALLY happening behind the footlights of a play. To a Negro the words "Iron Curtain" might be a wall ... a towering wall ... a wall so deep you could not go under it if you tried; so high you could not possibly scale it; so wide you could not go around it. This wall is ... prejudice.

" 'I, Negro, was born behind that wall ... or if you will, that "curtain." In time, because of constantly failing health, I wandered into the dog game as an outlet for my desire for clean, wholesome, good-natured athletic competition. The day I started with the dogs was the most fortunate day of my existence. I have learned through the years, and have come to realize with tremendous appreciation, that the dogs, as trite as it may seem to some, have brought me more pleasure and freedom than anything else in the world. I have discovered to my amazement and pleasure that 'dog-people' have accepted me as a 'friend' in the true sense of the word. Dogs, odd as it may seem, have opened up doors for me that would have always been closed; by the magic of their influence, the oft-sneered-at word, "Democracy" has taken on a real, lasting, beautiful meaning for me and my wife.'

"Tragically, it all came to an end in 1957, at age 64; upon his death from metastasized stomach cancer (which he diagnosed himself). Chances are Dr. McCain would have been a successful breeder, exhibitor, and judge in any time period, but given the fact that he was so successful in an era when everything should have been against him ... yet wasn't ... is clearly remarkable. Not only was he brilliant, but he was an extraordinarily talented and kind man, way ahead of his time!"

I'm certain Dr. McCain would concur with Hannah's words, "Dreams aren't always impossible. Some of us just have to work harder to make 'em come true."